An Awful Cat-titude

Meow for Murder #1

Addison Moore

and

Bellamy Bloom

Edited by Paige Maroney Smith
Cover by Lou Harper, Cover Affairs
Published by Hollis Thatcher Press, LTD.

Copyright © 2020 by Addison Moore, Bellamy Bloom

This novel is a work of fiction. Any resemblance to peoples either living or deceased is purely coincidental. Names, places, and characters are figments of the author's imagination. The author holds all rights to this work. It is illegal to reproduce this novel without written expressed consent from the author herself.

All Rights Reserved.

Books

By

Addison Moore

&

Bellamy Bloom

Cozy Mysteries

Meow for Murder
An Awful Cat-titude (Meow for Murder #1)
A Dreadful Meow-ment (Meow for Murder 2)

Country Cottage Mysteries
Kittyzen's Arrest (Country Cottage Mysteries 1)
Dog Days of Murder (Country Cottage Mysteries 2)
Santa Claws Calamity (Country Cottage Mysteries 3)
Bow Wow Big House (Country Cottage Mysteries 4)
Murder Bites (Country Cottage Mysteries 5)

Books By Addison Moore

Cozy Mysteries

Murder in the Mix

Cutie Pies and Deadly Lies (Murder in the Mix 1)
Bobbing for Bodies (Murder in the Mix 2)
Pumpkin Spice Sacrifice (Murder in the Mix 3)
Gingerbread and Deadly Dread (Murder in the Mix 4)
Seven-Layer Slayer (Murder in the Mix 5)
Red Velvet Vengeance (Murder in the Mix 6)
Bloodbaths and Banana Cake (Murder in the Mix 7)
New York Cheesecake Chaos (Murder in the Mix 8)
Lethal Lemon Bars (Murder in the Mix 9)
Macaron Massacre (Murder in the Mix 10)
Wedding Cake Carnage (Murder in the Mix 11)
Donut Disaster (Murder in the Mix 12)
Toxic Apple Turnovers (Murder in the Mix 13)
Killer Cupcakes (Murder in the Mix 14)
Pumpkin Pie Parting (Murder in the Mix 15)
Yule Log Eulogy (Murder in the Mix 16)
Pancake Panic (Murder in the Mix 17)
Sugar Cookie Slaughter (Murder in the Mix 18)

Devil's Food Cake Doom (Murder in the Mix 19)
Snickerdoodle Secrets (Murder in the Mix 20)
Strawberry Shortcake Sins (Murder in the Mix 21)
Cake Pop Casualties (Murder in the Mix 22)
Flag Cake Felonies (Murder in the Mix 23)
Peach Cobbler Confessions (Murder in the Mix 24)

1

"*I don't want to die!*" The words rip from my throat as if they were being pulled out with barbed wire.

My name is Stella Santini. I've got long black hair, light brown eyes, stand at an average height of five-foot-five, and I can see the future.

Okay, fine.

Confession: I'm no psychic. Nor have I ever come close to predicting what the future might hold—not with any accuracy anyway.

You see, ever since I was a little girl, I had what my Nana Rose liked to call the shakes. Technically, it's more of a shiver, and when you get down to it, there's a warm, fuzzy feeling involved that makes me want to forget about the world around me for a moment and retreat to the dark recesses of my mind where a thought plays out like a movie and I *see things*.

And trust me when I say, I have been wrong about interpreting the things I see on more than one occasion.

Take now for instance. This morning when a scene from the West End Woods flashed through my mind and I saw myself running for my life—I thought maybe I might be running from a serial killer looking for his next victim on this odd jaunt through the woods or running from a bear looking for his first meal post-hibernation, thus the solemn decision I came to during my second cup of coffee to stay the heck away from the West End Woods for the duration of my supernatural life.

But in a twist that only fate could provide, here I am, a mere hour later, panting, ducking evergreen trees and their prickly branches that threaten to poke my eyes out as if my life were on the line, and, oddly enough, I think it is.

"Don't kill me!" I howl once again, ducking and jiving my way through the forest as my Uncle Vinnie chases me through the woods with a bona fide weapon in his hand.

"I'm not gonna kill you for God's sake!" he riots right back.

"Then why are you holding a gun?"

Let's backtrack for a minute. After I enjoyed my *third* cup of coffee this morning, Uncle Vinnie called and said I had fifteen minutes to get dressed because we had things to discuss and he was picking me up pronto.

He sounded serious, morbid even. And I know him well enough to realize he meant business. I had an inkling about the subject he was going to prick. I happen to be what the mob likes to call a dead girl walking. Less than twenty-four hours ago, in what I and any sane person would call a very unfortunate chain of events, I managed to tick off the mob, the federal government, and break up with my idiot boyfriend of two years, Johnny Rizzo, all within a fifteen-minute span. And judging by this mad dash through the West End Woods, you could toss my Uncle Vinnie on that ticked-off list, too.

My foot catches on a buckling root system and I trip, slowing myself down enough for me to know I've just widened that bullseye on my back.

"Don't shoot!" I cry out, jogging to a finish as I spin around.

Uncle Vinnie stops within feet of me, panting, the veins on his neck throbbing like a couple of angry garden snakes about to wiggle their way into his brain.

Uncle Vinnie is tall, with black hair, dark eyes, and bushy eyebrows that hover over his face, giving him that perpetually angry look he's got going for him in life. But, by and large, he's a good guy who stepped up to the plate once my father was put away five years ago on RICO charges. He treated my brother, sister, and me as if we were his own children while my mother got a quickie divorce and began to chase men far younger straight into her bedroom.

"Please," I beg. "Put down the gun."

"What?" He squints over at me. "What the heck are you talking about? This ain't no gun." He shoves something toward me and I turn my head in horror.

It's not unusual for a man of my uncle's standing within the organization to take care of his own once word gets out that their proverbial number is up. And by *take care of*, I mean bump off the planet in a far more humane method than the fate that awaits them otherwise. And that's exactly why I suspect my Uncle Vinnie has dragged me out to this isolated strip of nature just outside of Hastings, New Jersey, the town in which I was born and raised.

He's brought me here to die. My loving uncle is about to impart what the *family* refers to as a *mercy execution*.

"It's not a gun?" I stagger for a moment. "You mean you're going to *stab* me to death? My God, how could you?

Is that any way to treat a girl you said you regarded as a daughter when your own brother went to prison?"

He blinks back, stunned. "Stella, look in my hand," he growls as he rattles the instrument of death my way once again. "It's a box of hair dye."

"Oh God, you're going to poison me?" I bury my face in my hands a moment. "Do you even realize how painful that will be? How much worse do you really think it will be for me at the hand of the Morettis?"

Ten years ago, after my father single-handedly unraveled the entire Fazio family in a mere weekend, the Morettis took over all of New Jersey with an iron fist, and one of their underlings happened to be my ex, Johnny Rizzo.

Johnny is the one that dragged me into that whole let's screw the Morettis scheme while they screw the government. It involved a car wash, a donut shop, a chop shop, dirty money, and a monster profit that's kept me in Louis Vuitton bags for the past six months, but the inner workings of Johnny's idiotic scheme are far too complicated to dig into at the moment, nor do I care to relive them.

But my dad... I've spent the last five years reliving everything about that man. How I loved the way things were before everything fell apart.

My father, Angelo Santini, or The Sunday Sinner as he's since been dubbed, is in prison on RICO charges. Prior to his incarceration, he became an informant for the feds. He wore a wire, the whole nine-weasel yards—and on a Sunday no less, thus his dishonorable new title.

Suffice it to say, he's as good as dead if he ever gets out—and maybe on the inside, too.

My dad cut a deal. Not a good deal. The feds still managed to seize everything, from our small kitchen appliances to my mother's minks. Yes, real minks had been sacrificed to create those furry horrors my mother loved to ensconce herself in no matter if the weather dictated their presence or not. Believe me, she is no friend of PETA.

But as soon as the government licked us clean, she was filing for divorce and out on the cougar prowl. Her preference for men younger than her own children is still something I can't wrap my head around.

In less than twenty-four hours after my father's incarceration, our first-class world turned into a third-world nightmare.

It turns out, Dad and his buddies were smuggling millions of dollars' worth of drugs into the country, via Latin America, and the Fazio family distributed it right here in New Jersey.

But since Daddy's little tap dance with the wire, that nightmare with the Fazios imploding and the Morettis stepping up to take their place led to my own aforementioned nightmare called Johnny Rizzo. And it was his bright idea to steal from the mob, which accidentally tipped off the feds to the Morettis' felonious misgivings—that led me here, to my very own execution party sponsored by Clairol.

"Stella," Uncle Vinnie barks my name out as if he were trying to wake me from a very bad dream, and how I wish he were. "I'm not going to kill you. I'm doing you a favor. The Morettis have already decided they want you quiet." In the mob, *quiet* is code for dead. "Johnny took off last night or they'd have gotten him first."

"He took off?" My eyes bulge at the thought. "And he left me here to fry?" Okay, confession: technically, Johnny isn't my ex quite yet. As of yesterday, we were still together. I haven't actually had the privilege of slapping him silly and telling him to take a hike just yet, only because we knew our lives were about to implode in far more dramatic ways than any mere breakup could bring on.

But on my way home from that fiasco, I had broken up with him a thousand times in my head. I came this close to texting him with the news but didn't want to deny myself the pleasure of looking him in the eye when I did it—and I might have been looking forward to shoving my knee into his crotch as well.

Johnny Rizzo promised me a rose garden and instead wrapped me in thorns and threw me into a sewer.

"Yes, he took off." Uncle Vinnie nods aggressively as if this should have been obvious. "You're on your own, kid. And I'm not going to kill you." His features soften. "I'm going to help you." He hands me the box with a picture of a redhead on the front who could double as Ariel from *The Little Mermaid*. "I've got a car waiting around the corner. Sit in the back. You'll find a large envelope filled with the paperwork you're going to need. New driver's license, Social Security card, passport, and car insurance. Everything you need to start a new life. My driver is taking you up to the New York border. I bought a car for you. It's not much, but it's yours. There's some gas money in the glove compartment. You'll have to be smart about how you spend it. Drive through New York, then up through Vermont until you get to Canada." He swipes the phone out of my hand. "In the glove compartment you'll also find a burner phone. I've got the number. I'll be calling from a burner myself. You don't call anybody else, you hear?"

"What? Give me that." I dive for my phone, but he tosses it to the ground and quickly puts a bullet through it before putting his gun back into his pocket. "This is really happening?" Tears sting my eyes as I look to the man I've regarded as a second father for my entire life.

"It's really happening." His eyes grow glossy as well. "Goodbye, Stella. That's the last time I will ever say your name, and the last time you'll hear it. You got that?"

My head wobbles back and forth. "What's my new name?" I swallow hard to keep from bawling like a baby.

"Bowie Binx, with an X."

"Bowwow *what*?" I snip, highly annoyed that I had no say in this. "Are you kidding me? I've waited my whole life to crawl from under the name my parents gifted me and you did what to me now?"

"Bowie Binx." He shrugs. "What can I say? I was working under a very tight time constraint. You have no idea how hard it was to put together a fictitious life in less than twenty-four hours."

"Bowie Binx." I try it on for size. "How in the heck did you come up with that whopper?"

"I happened to be listening to some good music. David Bowie was playing at the time, and I went with it. And as for

Binx, I asked Minnie what she wanted to name her next kitten and it's the first thing that flew from her lips."

Minnie is Uncle Vinnie's thee-year-old granddaughter who thinks she's married to her stepfather because her mother, my cousin Jackie, thought it would be cute to have him put a ring on her finger, too, during their wedding ceremony.

"Great. I'm named after a legendary singer and an imaginary cat. I couldn't have done better myself."

"You keep up with the sharp tongue, little lady. You're going to need it to survive. It's a tough world out there. Even in Canada." He wags a finger my way. "You'll see how cold and unfeeling it is without the warm, strong arms of the family around you."

"Yeah, well, the family wants me dead. I think I'll take my chances with a bunch of cold, unfeeling Canadians." I suck in my bottom lip as I look to my uncle for what feels like the very last time. "I love you."

"I know." He pulls me in and holds me for a small eternity, and I truly do feel the warm, strong arms of family around me. "If the burner phones don't work out, we'll find another way to communicate. The code word is *meow*."

I make a face. "Another contribution from Minnie?"

He gives a somber nod.

And then, just like that, he turns me around and instructs me to run.

And run I do.

Heigh-ho, heigh-ho, it's off to Canada I go.

Let's hope I don't run into Johnny Rizzo there or I'll kill him.

And that's one prognostication I can guarantee will come true.

2

The envelope Uncle Vinnie left me was smaller than I imagined.

The driver of the dark sedan was stoic and quiet as a church mouse as he drove me to the state line. I asked him a million questions on the way over and he ignored every single one. I'm betting Uncle Vinnie made him take an oath of silence. And seeing that the Santini men are prone to secretly recording auditory events, my Uncle Vinnie was probably taping the entire one-sided conversation, just in case he needed to fire a bullet into this poor man's skull.

The driver pulls up alongside a beat-up red Honda hatchback that looks to be from another millennium entirely and hitches his thumb for me to get out.

The hatchback is more of a rust color than it is a cherry red. The seats have long gashes running through them intermittently, letting me know this tub of steel was witness to a violent crime at some point in time. There's cash in the glove compartment just like Uncle Vinnie said there would be, along with that burner phone. The old car sputters and kicks as we make our way through endless desolate highways, and I reflect on all I've left behind.

My mother, Marie Santini, most likely won't know I'm gone until at least next week when she comes looking to borrow another one of my Louis Vuitton bags. She likes to cycle through them about every seven days and she just borrowed one yesterday. And as it stands, she's officially now the owner of the entire collection whether she knows it or not.

I have a brother and a sister, too.

My brother, Lorenzo, is twenty-nine. He's older than me by one year. He works down on the waterfront as a mechanic, and between work and his hypersexual love life, he may not notice I'm missing for a solid year.

My sister, Stephanie, younger by one year, works at her boyfriend's mother's nail salon and I feel as if I haven't seen her for a solid year. Once her feet outgrew my shoe size, she outgrew the practicality for a sister like me. Steph and I have never been close, but that doesn't mean I didn't crave it. I craved a lot of things, and almost all of them revolved around a normal family whose definition didn't include anything about a hierarchy of leg breakers.

The red beast I'm driving coughs and sputters her way halfway through New York before I decide to duck into a Denny's and scarf down a couple of scrambled eggs and a heap of bacon even though it's well past dinnertime. Once I'm through inhaling my food, I duck into their restroom and run that box of dye Uncle Vinnie gifted me through my hair, contemplating how I went from being a pampered princess to a fugitive on the run.

Not surprisingly, the hair dye doesn't take. It looks less Ariel the mermaid and more like I ran a can of Cherry Coke through my tresses. The red rim of dye along my forehead isn't so flattering either. As if my failure to conceal my appearance wasn't enough, I ripped a hole in the back of my yoga pants as I struggled to pull them up after I used the restroom.

I bang my head against the stall for a good long while. I've never been a horseshoe, but then I've never been such a magnet for bad luck either. Something tells me any luck I did have just ran out for good. And I flush the toilet to cement this theory.

I hop back into the red catastrophe I've nicknamed Wanda. Roadkill was a more appropriate moniker, but I had the sneaking suspicion it wouldn't be wise in the event my supernatural powers decided to manifest themselves in a whole new direction.

We hit the highway again until my vision grows blurry and my long blinks start turning into short naps, so I pull over and curl into a fetal position until the sun comes up and screams for me to move again.

I yawn to life as I drive out of New York and into Vermont. Winter just turned to spring and I can't help but take in the beauty of the verdant fields dotted in honeysuckle and bluebells.

I'm just about to crest the Canadian border when Wanda starts to sputter again. This time she's blowing out steam and all of the gauges on the dashboard are spinning every which way at once, so I do exactly what she's telling me to do—get the heck off the highway before she blows up.

"Next exit, Starry Falls, Vermont," I read as the highway turns into a thicket of woods on either side of me until low and behold a small blip of a town percolates to life and I end up on Main Street in hopes of spotting a mechanic's shop. Heck, at this point I'd take a veterinarian's office. A rabies shot or two, and Wanda just might be good to go.

Then in a rather unceremonious burst, Wanda lets out a loud whistling scream and a rather obnoxious series of claps that don't sound all that different from one of my brother's flatulent episodes. She gives a hard jerk and I pull her to the side of the road where she rolls to a sputtering finish.

"She's dead." I smack the steering wheel. "No, no, no, you can't be dead. You can't leave me in Podunk, Vermont to die along with you. We've got to get to Canada. We made a pact, remember?"

Okay, so we didn't make a pact.

I pull forward the envelope Uncle Vinnie left me and shove my new bevy of IDs into one of the zipped pockets of my Lululemon running jacket and I grab the rest of the gas money and shove it into my other pocket. It takes great pains to uncoil myself from the driver's seat. Every muscle in my body is sore and stiff from last night's impromptu slumber party with the newly deceased automobile.

A crisp breeze hits me where the sun shouldn't shine, and I quickly tie my jacket around my waist to hide my newly acquired ripped seam. No use in scaring off the residents just yet. I'll save that fun for later when the feds come at me with their weapons drawn.

I head out and stagger my way down the innocent street lined with a happy looking yarn shop, a candy store, a realty office, a rundown diner, and a Chinese joint. There's an Italian restaurant across the street, a post office, an aerobic studio, and yet there's not a single auto mechanic in sight.

The streets are lined with rows of maple trees with their branches full of young spring shoots a brilliant shade of green. I look down as far as my eye can see and spot two rather odd sights that force me to blink in the event I'm hallucinating.

The first is a gray stone structure that looks as if it could easily dwarf any of the buildings lining the street. It sits crooked on a tiny hill and has a haunted mansion appeal. It's clearly out of place and has that whole I-was-just-plucked-from-the-English-countryside-and-dropped-from-the-sky look about it. It's either a castle or a mansion and it sits at the end of Main Street with a sign staked out front, but I'm too far to read it.

The second odd sight is what's nestled in the hillside behind the overgrown structure. A gorgeous set of double-tiered waterfalls stands proud, rushing with white streams of glittering liquid that never seems to end.

My feet zoom in the direction of the overgrown stone building, and soon I'm close enough I spot an entire legion of cats napping on the lawn out front, dripping down the porch, and nestled in just about every window that faces the street. Cats of every shape and size, white, brown, orange, striped, spotted, angry looking, innocent looking, and a few that look as if they're plotting to eat me for breakfast.

A tan cat with both spots and stripes bravely traipses my way and juts its head out demanding to be petted.

"Oh, aren't you sweet," I whisper as I do just that. "Something tells me this is your circus and these are your adorable monkeys. As soon as I get something in my belly, I'm going to roll around on the lawn with all of you and see if I can make any new furry friends. God knows you can't be any cattier than the friends I left behind."

A sign up ahead catches my attention. *Mortimer Manor— good coffee, good food, and more! Head on into the café!*

"Coffee," the word hums out of me like a groan from the pit of my very being. "*Coffee.*"

The sound of female voices escalating comes from somewhere inside the structure, but I'm undeterred. Yelling is my family's love language. No matter how loud it gets, it won't scare me away. If anything, it'll draw me near and make me homesick in the process.

A brass sign sits in front of the door that holds a poster with the picture of a decent looking guy in a ten-gallon hat holding a guitar. It reads *Welcome country crooner Perry Flint, Friday night at seven! Tickets sold at the door.*

A couple of cathedral-style double doors sit open and welcome me inside. It's cool in here. It holds the scent of cloying perfume and bacon, an unnerving combination if ever there was one.

The interior is rife with dark wood and deep crimson carpeting with some sort of a navy paisley pattern that eats at my eyes. There's a grand foyer and an even grander entry and it looks as if there are signs staked in front of the cavernous rooms that lie ahead. But I'm not interested in venturing off in that direction. Instead, I follow the sign that promises me one-dollar coffee.

Up ahead, a glass door opens, amplifying the sounds of that raucous argument, and out speeds a body that quickly slams into me and I sail back, staggering and moaning as I struggle to keep from falling.

"Whoa," a deep voice strums as a pair of strong arms wrap themselves around my waist, and before I know it, I'm looking into a pair of light blue eyes rimmed with navy, giving them that Siberian husky appeal, and for a moment in time I forget about the mob, the feds, my idiot ex, and Wanda my dead Honda and swoon directly into those magical peepers. The rest of him isn't so bad either. His dark hair and the appropriate amount of stubble peppering his cheeks highlight the fact he's brutally handsome.

He leans in and gasps. "*Geez*," he belts it out as he takes a full step back. "My God, are you bleeding?"

"What?" I lean over and inspect my reflection in the glass door before me, and what stares back has me gasping in horror as well.

"Oh no." I groan at the sight of myself. My hair is rising to the sky, disheveled and matted. My mascara has run down to my nose and there's a red ring staining the skin that circles my hairline, giving off the effect of a head wound. "Oh God. How is this my life?"

"Are you okay?" The man wastes no time in pulling out his phone. "I'll call the paramedics."

"No!" I practically dive for his phone and he quickly holds it up over my head. "I'm not bleeding. I dyed my hair in a Denny's last night, and as you can see, I had a little bit of a runoff." I pat my forehead. "Hey, do you live here? I'm kind of homeless at the moment, and believe me when I say being homeless is a heck of a lot harder than it looks. I had to spend the night in Wanda last night. That's the death trap my uncle gave me, but she's dead now and I'm carless *and* houseless and I only have enough cash to keep me in hot coffee for thirteen days. You wouldn't happen to know where I could spend the night on the cheap, would you?"

He leans back as if he suddenly found me repulsive, and it's only then I note his dark suit, that plain navy tie, and the fresh scent of his thick cologne. Leave it to me to find the town hottie and stumble in front of him like the queen of hobos.

"No." He smacks his lips as the shouting rises from inside.

"No? How about a job? I have a feeling I'm going to need to scrape together a few nickels and dimes to get Wanda back up on four wheels, if you know what I mean."

The sound of dishes breaking erupts from inside the café and he nods that way. "Something tells me they'll be hiring a brand new manager in just a few minutes."

The door bursts open and a disheveled brunette stalks out with her hair falling out of a bun, her red lipstick smeared over her cheek, and the look of hellfire in her eyes.

Nice to know I'm not the only brunette having a hell of a week.

"You!" she shouts, jabbing her finger at the man in the suit. "I'll see you tonight." She takes off in a huff, and I can't help but giggle.

"Something tells me you like 'em rough and rowdy." I give a cheeky wink.

He frowns a moment before picking up a briefcase I never quite saw him set down.

He nods my way. "What's your name?"

"Ste—*Bowie*. Bowie Bing—Bingham? No, that's not right." I squeeze my eyes shut tight a moment. "Binx!" I raise a fist as if calling out the correct answer on a quiz show.

"Bowie Binx." His cheek curls on one side. "Do you need me to call anyone for you? Where are you from?"

"No!" I'm quick to stop up the dam before it truly bursts. "I'm from—Chicago. I drove all day yesterday and my car just died out of the blue."

He tips his head to the side, inspecting me with those soulful eyes. "It only took you one night to drive here from Illinois?"

"Did I say Illinois?" A high-pitched laugh bubbles from me. "I meant Chicago... *Connecticut*."

"Chicago, Connecticut?" He gives a long blink.

Shoot.

"Oh yeah, it's a small town. So small it's not even on the map." A nervous titter evicts from my throat. "Google Earth didn't even waste its time with us, we're that unimportant. So do you know of a place to stay?"

"I'm sorry." He shakes his head. "Good luck with the job," he says as he takes off.

"I didn't get your name!" I shout, but he's already outside, pretending he didn't hear me.

I guess it's true what they say. The minute you start living on the streets, you're invisible to the rest of society—especially hot men with briefcases.

It takes everything in me to venture into that café with my wild hair, my staccato zombie walk, and overall air of a degenerate nature. It's light and bright inside, not a single customer in sight. The tables are evenly dispersed, the wooden floors look as if they've been clawed by a thousand cats, and there's a chipped counter up front with a couple of women standing behind. The tables are beat up, the booths and chairs are made from ripped up red Naugahyde and duct tape, and there's a black and white checkered wallpaper border that looks as if it's doing its best not to fall right off the walls.

I make my way to the two women standing near the counter. One is older than my mother but not quite as old as Nana Rose was when she passed.

Her silver hair is cut in a blunt bob and she has on a shock of dark red lipstick, lots of dark kohl lining her bright green eyes, and she has an overall soured expression about her. She's wearing a crushed velvet blazer in gun metal gray and has a brooch in the shape of an overgrown ladybug that cinches her blouse at the neck.

The younger one looks about my age, a bit more hardened by life, brown hair with thick, chunky blonde highlights, boobs bustling out of her unbuttoned blouse, and a pretty face, or at least it would be if she wasn't busy scowling at me like I was about to rob the place.

"This is a stickup," the words bark out of me, partially because I couldn't help it and partially because what the heck. I'm already fumbling around in some alternate universe. How much worse can it get?

The two of them exchange a glance, and for a solid moment I'm convinced the register drawer is about to fly open. But instead, they burst into laughter and I plop down on the stool in front of them, failing at yet another criminal area in life.

"All right, clown," the older one drawls the words out, and if I'm not mistaken, with some sort of unidentified accent. It's sort of a cross between an English accent and a hard-nosed socialite. "What are you really doing here? Would you like the breakfast special, perhaps?"

The younger one shakes her head. "We don't have a breakfast special."

The older one hushes her in haste and already I like the two of them.

"I heard you were hiring." I swallow hard as I look to the two of them. "The man with the suit and briefcase told me so." I hitch my thumb to the door and they look twice as baffled. "The hot guy with the icy blue eyes?"

The younger one waves me off. "That's just Shep."

Shep. Now there's a name that practically guarantees he won't be allowed in a single mob family and I like him more because of it.

The older woman leans in. "Do you know Shep? Is he recommending you? Have you worked in food service before?"

"Oh yeah, lots of times." If serving my brother and my idiot ex grilled cheese sandwiches at their beck and call for years counts for anything, I'm a seasoned pro. Not to mention my quasi-illegal stint at the donut shop. "So when can I start?"

The older woman ticks her head to the younger girl and they seem to be having some sort of a silent conversation.

The older woman plucks a dirty apron off the counter and tosses it my way.

"How about now?"

"You mean I'm hired as a waitress?" I quickly pull the apron over my head and the frilly thing fans out over my chest.

"Nope." The younger woman comes around the counter and plucks the apron off and ties it around my waist. "You're the new manager."

"Manager?" I swallow hard. "Wow, that's great. I think. So what are your names?"

No paperwork? No questions regarding my head wound? Why do I get the feeling I just got handed the hot potato of managerial positions?

My God, I'll have access to those registers myself in less than an hour. But something tells me the spare change rolling around in there isn't worth risking the pokey for.

The older woman presses out a crimson smile. "I'm Opal Mortimer and this is waitress extraordinaire, Tilly Teasdale."

I wince to the younger woman at the mention of her unfortunate last name. Things couldn't have been easy in school for her.

Tilly juts her chin forward. "And who are you?"

"Bowie Binx," I answer just as the door to the café bursts open and a teenage girl with a long ponytail and cat-winged eyes flies to the counter next to me.

"*Mom*," she barks at Tilly. "I need six bottles of Jamison, two kegs, and a couple of cases of peppermint schnapps. It's Friday and we're having a party at Amanda's."

"We don't serve that here"—Tilly leans back, the look of boredom quickly taking over her features—"and you're sixteen." She folds her arms across her chest and her cleavage bursts forth with the threat of unleashing from any harness-like device she has restraining them.

"Hey, you owe me!" The girl doesn't waste any time in escalating the situation.

"Owe you for what?" Tilly snaps back.

"For the time you pretended to be a seventeen-year-old boy from Manhattan looking to hook up. Only a sick person makes their kid fall in love with an imaginary hottie. You're not buying, are you?"

Tilly shakes her head as she looks my way. "Boobie, this is my daughter, Jessie. Please ignore the tantrum she's throwing. I don't buy liquor for minors." She gives the girl a wink like maybe she does.

"It's Bowie," I whisper, but Boobie feels about right considering where I've ended up in life, so I don't make a stink about correcting her.

"Fine," the girl snips. "I saw Regina screaming on the front lawn. I'll ask *her*. She hates you enough to do it, too." She charges for the door.

"Hey!" Tilly shouts after her. "Have her pick me up a couple of six packs while you're at it!"

My mouth falls open. As I live and breathe, I had no idea there were places in the world that could give my hometown a run for its dysfunctional money.

I hitch my thumb toward the door. "Is Regina the girl that ran out screaming?"

Opal nods. "That would be her. Regina Valentine."

"Are she and Shep a thing?" I'm not even sure why I asked. "I mean, she said something about seeing him later tonight, but it kind of sounded like a threat." And it kind of sounded like a date all at the same time. A part of me respects women who can pull off a feat like that. Something tells me she'd fit in nicely in Jersey.

Opal chortles. "Yes, well, she's definitely his type."

Tilly rolls her eyes. "Everyone is Shep's type. Have they knocked boots? Maybe. Shep does love the ladies."

Opal offers a sorrowful look my way. "You'll get sick of him soon enough. He uses this place like an office. So where are you from? Where are you staying?"

Tilly leans in. "You're new in town, aren't you?" There's a dazed look in her eyes as if she's seeing a slab of fresh meat—me.

I'm about to answer when an all too familiar warm, fuzzy feeling takes over and spreads throughout my limbs, rendering me disabled for a moment. The room blinks in and out of focus as I get a serious bout of tunnel vision. And in my mind's eye, I see Opal looking at me with fright as a gun dangles from her fingers. *"Oh my God,"* she says. *"He's dead."*

The room snaps back into focus and a cool breeze washes over me as Opal shakes me by the shoulders.

"Oh, for goodness' sake, Tilly, get the girl a chocolate chip cookie. She nearly passed out."

"No." I shake my head as I look to the sweet, somewhat kooky older woman beside me. "I saw something. You were standing there with a gun and you said, 'oh my God, he's dead.'" I glance to Tilly then Opal. "Look, I'll leave town. On foot apparently. But sometimes I see things, and I think you're too nice to do some serious time. Don't do it. Whoever this man is, he's not worth wearing an orange jumpsuit for life." I should know, I'm working hard to avoid the same wardrobe malfunction.

Tilly makes a wheezing sound as she comes in close. "You're one of those psychics, aren't you? The kind they advertise at two in the morning? What's going to happen to me tonight? Am I getting lucky with Perry Flint?"

"What? No, I'm not a psychic. That's horrible stuff. It's witchcraft. It's from the devil. Believe me, I know. I'm just—" I pause long enough to decide there's no point in spilling all the supernatural beans. "I'm just a girl who sometimes sees things, and it gets me in trouble more often than not. And please do me a favor. Don't tell anyone." I look Opal in the eye. "And whatever you do, don't kill him."

3

It turns out, this rickety old café really does have customers.

Lots of them.

In fact, it has a healthy staff, too, that consists of four cooks and three waitresses. Not to mention me—the oddball out calling the shots. Although, in what's turned into a bit of a surprise, nobody actually listens to me.

Tilly stands in the corner, filing her nails over the food that's waiting to be delivered to the tables at hand.

There's a guy named Mud Miller, who is more or less the handyman at the manor but occasionally pinch-hits with the customers. Currently, he's doing a majority of the waiting and the bussing, while the other waitresses play on their phones and argue with their boyfriends.

Mud is tall and scrawny and has a sharp aversion to food touching on the plate even if he's not actually going to eat the food. He's got choppy, short, blond hair that looks as if a vengeful ex-girlfriend attacked him with scissors in the dark. But he's got a good game face with the customers and a mischievous twinkle in his eyes that makes me feel as if he's going to be a natural ally.

"Ooh." Tilly takes off her apron. "It's time to go. Perry Flint is probably taking the stage as we speak. Come on, Bowser. You won't want to miss this one."

"Bowie." I shoot her a look as I glance around the café. "And I can't go. The sign says we close at nine. That's two more hours of torture for me."

Tilly clucks her tongue, her watery blue eyes pinned right to mine. "You don't have to close. You're the manager. Make one of the peons do it. That's how Regina did it."

"Shouldn't I count out the register?"

"That's what we got Mud for."

I glance down. I've already counted out the cash drawer ten times.

All right, so I was eyeing those greenbacks in an effort to scoop them up and run like heck. And believe me, if

Wanda was feeling better, I would have. But with no car, and no mechanic to work a miracle, it looks as if I'm stuck at the catnip café. Honest to God, there have been at least a half dozen adorable felines sniffing around the door outside just begging to be let in.

"I'll be there in a minute," I say. "Can I ask what the deal is with all the cats around here? Did someone dump a can of tuna on the carpet outside? Because for the life of me, I can't seem to figure out what's going on."

Tilly chuckles as she waves me off. "Opal is Starry Falls' resident certified crazy cat lady."

"*Oh*," I drawl the word out as the message comes in clear. "I get it. My Nana Rose loved cats, too. She had three before she passed away."

Tilly rolls her eyes. "Yeah, well, Opal's got your granny beat. She has at least three *hundred*. She has a trough she feeds them from out back every night. And at about four o'clock she starts what she calls her kitty run." She leans in. "The trunk of her car is loaded with kitty kibble. And she drives to at least six different locations and scatters food in bulk. People hate her for it. They say it's a nuisance." She shrugs. "I say let the poor woman have at it. Cats are one of the few things that give her pleasure anymore."

"Anymore? What happened?"

"First, her husband left her for the baton girl in the Fourth of July freedom parade out in Sterling Lake, then he was arrested for tax evasion and securities fraud. He's out now and doing pretty good again, but he kicked Opal to the curb. Opal was once a fat cat herself, and now all she has left in this world is this dump."

"This *dump*? This dump is basically a mansion in the event you haven't noticed."

Tilly shakes her head. "It's plagued with problems, and it keeps sucking what little money she does have out of her. She refuses to take in boarders. And she tries to bilk the townspeople for all they're worth whenever she can, but she's no good at it. She's lost everything but the cashmere sweater off her back, and the feds are constantly breathing down her neck."

"Wow. Opal and I really have a lot in common."

Tilly blinks my way.

"I mean, we've both fallen on tough times." Not to mention that whole feds and lousy ex thing. "Hey! Do you think Opal would let me spend the night here? I have nowhere else to go."

She lifts her brows as she links her arm to mine. "Why don't we go ask her, little miss."

Tilly leads us through the manor, which is now teeming with bodies as everyone struggles to cram themselves into a set of double doors in the back.

We weave our way through the crowd, and soon enough we're in a cavernous ballroom, dimly lit with pink and yellow spotlights twirling up above. There's a bona fide stage up front with a giant framed poster that reads *Welcome Perry Flint!*

A single chair and a microphone sit on stage with a single white-hot spotlight over it.

It's elbow-to-elbow room only in this dance hall, and without putting too much effort into it, I spot Shep, the cranky walking suitcase, standing near the stage talking to a man with a cowboy hat, far too many teeth, and a smile that doesn't quit.

I'm about to point them out when Opal crops up wearing a houndstooth fitted blazer, a matching long skirt, black stilettos, and a hot pink scarf. Her silver hair is slightly frizzy yet curled under, and she's wearing that same dark lipstick she had on this afternoon.

"What do you think of the turnout?" Opal claps her hands softly to herself. "Every single person here paid ten dollars admittance." She looks my way. "They're collecting at the entrance to the manor. You can pay me later."

My mouth opens a moment. A part of me respects her hutzpah.

"I'm your employee," I point out. "And speaking of which, you wouldn't happen to have a room I can rent, do you? The only place I have to lay my head at night is my car." It might be spring, but given the fact the rear window won't roll all the way up, it makes for an icy night's sleep that I don't care to repeat.

"A room to rent?" Her penciled-in brows curl together. "I'm afraid the manor is full. I have a suite to myself, and the rest of the rooms are unavailable. I was fortunate enough to keep my entire winter collection and had to store them somewhere."

Tilly wrinkles her nose. "She's got a six room suite."

Opal waves her off before turning her attention back to me. "The car sounds wonderful, dear. I'm glad to know things are looking up for you." She starts to walk away and I block her.

"No, actually, they're not. Can I at least spend the night in the café? I'll curl up in a booth. And on the bright side, I won't be late for work."

She gasps as she looks to Tilly. "That's a wonderful idea! A twenty-four hour café. Why didn't you think of that?" She gives one of Tilly's chunky highlights a tug before putting in another earnest attempt of dissolving into the crowd, but I stand my ground.

"I hear you want to make some money off this joint." I tip my head her way. "Well, guess what, Opal? I'm your girl. I'll have you swimming in Benjamins by the end of the month or my name isn't Bowie Binx." It's not, but that's beside the point. "What do you say? Let me spend the night under that microscopic desk in the office? Or in your winter closet. Take your pick."

Pick the closet. Pick the closet.

Her ruby red lips twitch back and forth. "Fine, you can talk to Shep about his outhouse. Tell him it's a favor to me." She grunts as she looks to the ceiling. "I'd better see Mud about brewing some comfort pronto."

"Comfort?" I look to Tilly. Truthfully, it's the outhouse I should be questioning.

"It's code for something just a touch stronger," she says, navigating us through the crowd. "Come on, I can't wait to see the look on Shep's face when you ask if you can live in his outhouse. And more to the point, I can't wait until Perry Flint sees me." She pauses a moment to pull her blouse apart until a few more buttons loosen under the duress of her bosom.

We bump our way past bodies until we're standing before Shep, the man in the ten-gallon hat, and a leggy blonde curled up by his side.

Shep has ditched the suit for the night and traded it for jeans and a white T-shirt, his dark hair is slicked back, his stubble looks thicker, and those Siberian husky blue eyes take a moment to glare over at the two of us. A mob of women seems to be circling him, whispering amongst themselves while they work themselves into a fervor. He is a looker, I'll give him that.

"Hey"—Tilly gives a quick wave to the country crooner, clearly swooning in his midst—"I'm Tilly *Teasdale*." She lays a heavy emphasis on her last name, and now I'm starting to wonder whether or not we're both sporting fabricated monikers.

I lean in. "And I'm Bowie Binx." I blink a smile to the couple before me. The man of the hour has a rugged appeal with a carefully trimmed goatee and the aforementioned toothy grin. The girl is all curls and hot pink lips. Her body keeps gliding over his as if he were a greased pole she was riding for tips.

"Perry Flint." The man shakes both our hands. "And this here is my little lady, Devin O'Malley."

She shrugs. "Nice to meet you, girls. I'm just so proud of Perry. His song, 'Come Back to Me', just hit number one on the country charts this afternoon."

"Wow," I say. "Congratulations."

A dark-haired woman with a bun and black-rimmed glasses steps up. She's wearing a white buttoned-down blouse, black pencil skirt, and heels, and if we were at a club back home, I would have asked her for a vodka tonic even though I don't drink. Some things simply drive you there, and being homeless and on the run both qualify me to drink a bottle of vodka straight without stopping. Not that I would. With my preexisting supernatural condition, all sorts of things could and would go wrong with that scenario.

The brunette in the pencil skirt gives a shy smile to the blonde. "Devin, your brother just walked in."

Devin cranes her neck before squealing, "*Bud!*" She takes off and wraps her whole body around a man with a scraggly beard.

She sure looks happy to see her brother. The man looks a bit older than me, red hair, heavily etched crow's feet around his eyes, and I can't help but note his hands are riding up and down her back. It looks as if he's happy to see her, too.

Fun fact: I have never hugged my brother that way. But something tells me if I ever get to see him again I might just come close.

I make a face before turning back to the woman.

"You're on in ten minutes," she tells Perry as she irons out his plaid shirt with her hands. "Let's get you backstage."

He belts out a hearty chuckle. "Shep, girls, this is my personal assistant, Nicki. She's been keeping me in line for the last solid year. If it wasn't for her, I'd still be sleeping in the back of my car."

"We've got that in common," I mutter mostly to myself. "Nice to meet you, Nicki. I work here at the manor. I'm the manager of the café."

"Oh." She whips out a business card as thick as a matchbook and hands it to me. "Here's my number if you guys want to book him again. He's actually in demand until Christmas, but he always makes exceptions for shows close to home, so we can probably work something out."

"Great," I say, glancing to the card, and her name glints back at me in gold foil: Nicki Magnolia, personal assistant.

A tall gentleman with a shock of gray hair and a ruby-lipped smile leaps into our small circle.

"Hey-ho." He slaps Perry on the chest. "Hope you're not telling any tall tales about me." He gives a quick wink our way and his eyes make a pit stop at Tilly's bosom.

"Tilly Teasdale," she says it sultry while swaying her hips.

"Richard Broadman." He takes up her hand and kisses the back of it. "I'm the man in charge around here." He gives her a little wink. "If you're looking for someone to keep you in line, I'll be on call all evening."

Perry belts out a mournful laugh. "Ignore him. Richard is my manager. He's overworked."

"And underpaid," Richard adds while smacking Perry in the gut. He winks over at Tilly once again. "I meant what I said." The three of them take off in haste and a shudder rides through me.

"Don't even think about it, Tilly," I say. "You can't trust a man who winks twice in a thirty second time span. Not to mention the fact he was far more interested in what sits below your chin than above it."

"So what?" Her shoulders give a little bounce. "I like a man who knows how to focus on two of my finer points." She flashes a tight smile to Shep, and it has me wondering if he's focused on her finer points, too. "Hey, hey, Shepherd Pie.

You'll never guess who is spending the night in your outhouse."

Shep's T-shirt expands to unnatural widths with his next breath and my stomach squeezes tight.

He nods my way. "My apologies, Barley. I don't have an outhouse."

"*Bowie*," I say with a touch of irritation as I look to Tilly. "Why is that so hard to remember?"

Tilly shakes her head. "You don't get it, Shep. Opal wants you to do it as a favor to her before the poor girl tries to sleep in the back of the café."

Shep dips his chin a moment, and those lucent blue eyes set on mine before he turns to Tilly. "Take her to your place."

"What? No!" Tilly inches back as if he threatened her with roaches. "I've got"—she waves her hand—"a bit of a mess on my hands. And *company*. With any luck, I'll have Richard Broadman to entertain until the wee hours. No can do. She's the hot potato and Opal says you're it."

"What about your sofa?" I ask her, because apparently, I no longer have any qualms about inviting myself to spend the night where I'm clearly not wanted.

And hot potato? Well, hey, at least I'm hot.

AN AWFUL CAT-TITUDE

"Sorry." She tips her head to the side, her bottom lip pursed. "The sofa's sort of taken, too. That's for Jessie's boyfriends. They like to stay the night."

Great. I look back to Shep and the pink and yellow lights are hitting him just right, making him look monstrously handsome. It's safe to say I couldn't be trusted in that outhouse of his. I'm pretty sure I'd try to find his bedroom window and climb on in.

A pair of slender arms land around his chest and a brunette that looks vaguely familiar glides next to him with a cherry red smile budding on her lips.

"Looks like I haven't missed the party." She looks to Tilly. "I heard Opal filled my position with some homeless nutcase. Ten bucks says she robs the place and is gone by morning."

This must be Regina. She looks a touch more put together than I remember from this morning, but then, this entire day has been a bit of a blur. I shoot Shep the stink eye before ditching this trio. I'm on the hunt for the restroom, but my feet are twitching to make good on Regina's quasi-prophetic words.

I make a right toward the stage, down a narrow hall, and the rise of male voices garners my attention. I peer in that direction and spot Perry Flint having it out with a man a touch shorter than himself, prickly facial hair, and bug eyes that give him that crazy look people tend to stray from.

"I'm telling you now, you've gone too far," the man says while giving Perry a nice shove to the chest. "I'll make sure I get what's mine."

Perry nails the guy to the wall and leans in hard. "You better watch your back, boy."

A small gray cat slinks past me and lets out a rather quiet meow as if it didn't want any part of this action. And, believe you me, neither do I.

The man gives Perry a violent shove off of him. "*You* better watch *your* back."

He stalks off past me and Perry glances my way before disappearing through a door to the right.

In less than ten minutes, Perry takes the stage to the delight of a room full of swaying bodies. People are singing along, women are crying, underwear are tossed on stage, and I'd say the first set is a true blue hit.

Perry says a few words before heading off for a five-minute break and the house lights come up a notch.

Shep appears before me like a scowling dark shadow as the whites of his eyes glint over at me.

He rocks back on his heels, hands stuffed in his pockets. "So, how are you liking Starry Falls so far?"

"I don't," I say, trying to make my way past him, and he takes a step to the side, effectively blocking my path. "What's this? Are you trying to get lucky? Because I saw the way Regina was hanging all over you. I don't think she'd like her man scouting other prospects for the night, if you know what I mean."

His head cocks to the side, and that stern expression on his face only seems to harden.

"Regina and I aren't a couple. I just wanted to see if you figured out your situation for the night."

For a sweet, brief moment, I get lost in those mesmerizing eyes of his, but I know his type. Shep is far too handsome for his own good. And Lord knows I've played enough head games to realize to run the other way when I see a player like him on the horizon. But a part of me isn't convinced he's playing a game at all. And to be honest, that's a scarier prospect.

All my life, every man I've ever been with has lied to, swindled, or tried to control me. It's just a matter of figuring out which of the three this one wants to do.

"Don't worry, hot stuff. I'll be fine." I zip past him, on my way back to the restroom so I can bang my head against a stall for the duration of the night, but before I can get there, I bump into Opal.

"Bowie!" She nods my way. "Isn't this great? I think I'll ask to book him once a month—heck, once a week. At this rate, I might just be able to save up enough to go to Paris for the summer. Now wouldn't that be a hoot?"

"It's a hoot, all right," I say, lacking the proper Parisian enthusiasm.

"Oh"—she pouts to the opened door at the end of the hall—"I bet he went out that way."

I follow along and a tan fuzzy cat crosses our path, letting out a yowl of a scream.

A line of evergreens stands about thirty feet away, and a dirt patch sits just beyond the door. It's a dark night with nothing but a crescent moon and a spray of a thousand stars to light up the vicinity with a gentle blue cast.

Opal takes a few steps out and picks something up before turning my way.

"Oh my God," she says as her face bleaches out. "He's dead."

"Who's dead?" I gasp as I take the trinket out of her hand, only to find myself cradling a shiny black gun. I suck in a quick breath. "My vision!"

But before I can get too worked up about it, I spot a dark, lumpy object lying in the dirt just a few feet away. I stagger on over, and to my horror I see a man lying face up, a stream of dark liquid pooling around his chest.

"What's going on?" a male voice calls out from the manor, and I look over to see Shep striding my way.

He glances to the body before looking to the gun in my hand.

Perry Flint won't have to worry about singing his second set.

Perry Flint is dead.

And I just so happen to look pretty guilty.

4

I'm no expert, but standing over a man who has clearly breathed his last while holding what is presumed to be the murder weapon is hardly a good way to go undetected.

"Put down the weapon," Shep says it sternly as he whips something out from his waist, and the next thing I know I'm staring down the shiny barrel of a gun myself.

"Whoa," I say, lowering the firearm in my hand to the ground where it belongs.

Opal makes an odd squawking sound before she slaps Shep's arm silly.

"Would you put that thing away?" she shrills. "How many times do I have to tell you, this is not a shooting range? Valerie here was just taking the gun from me."

Bowie, I'm tempted to correct her, but I opt to keep my pie hole shut.

She tosses her hands in the air. "I thought it was a wallet. And once I realized what it was, it was too late. I was holding it, smothering it with my fingerprints. You don't think I'll do any hard time, do you?"

Shep lands his weapon back into that holster over his right hip and gives me a hard look.

"No, Opal, you're safe." He kneels by the victim and checks his vitals before rising and announcing that he's calling 911.

A couple steps out from the manor and heads this way.

The man steps into view and it's Richard, the white-haired steed Tilly was hoping to tame later tonight.

"What in the heck is going on? Have any of you seen Perry?" he asks before doing a double take and letting out a hard moan. "Nicki, you'd best get back inside. I don't think you should see this."

The woman with the tight bun does a little quick step in this direction and lets out a sharp cry at the sight before burying her head against Richard's chest.

"There, there." He shakes his head in Perry's direction. "Who could have predicted something so tragic?"

Not me, I want to say.

The wail of a siren cuts through the air, and in no time flat the place is crawling with sheriff's deputies with the words *Woodley County Sheriff's Department* written in large block letters on the back of their navy jackets.

"Oh my God," I mutter as I back away slowly. If I disappear now, I'll only look guilty, and yet every cell in my body is screaming *run*.

I glance to my left and spot a woman in tan pants and a navy blouse speaking with Opal. The woman has her phone out and appears to be taking notes and nodding. Her hair is pulled into a short ponytail, and from what I can tell, she looks as if she could grace the covers of magazines with her pouty lips and large dark eyes. Opal glances my way, and soon the two of them are headed over.

Shep steps up and blocks them from my view momentarily.

"Don't worry," he whispers. "If you're innocent, you have nothing to hide."

"*If?*" I can't help but gawk at him a moment as the two of them descend upon us. For as handsome as Shep is, he's equally annoying.

Opal sheds a ragged breath. "*Bodie*, this is Detective Grimsley. She'd like to speak with you about that gun incident." She leans in and whispers, "Don't say a word about you know what. The *vision*." She mouths those last two words. "I'm going to step inside now. Being near the dead gives me a stress rash." She bolts for the door, leaving that pouty-lipped brunette to observe me in a suspicious manner before she turns her attention to the undeniably comely man by my side.

Perfect. Shep can distract her with his man candy while I make a getaway.

"Shepherd Wexler." Her lips curl, but there's no smile attached to the effort. "Opal tells me you found the deceased."

My lips part as I look over at him.

He glances my way. "I found"—his eyes scan my features a moment—"this woman, Bowie, a friend of mine, holding the gun. It seems she came upon the scene and took the gun from Opal who picked it up off the floor to begin with."

Well, at least I wasn't the only one he threw under the bus.

"Bowie"—the woman looks my way—"I'm Detective Grimsley with the Woodley County Homicide Division. Just tell me the sequence of events, exactly how they occurred."

I quickly relay it all to her, starting from the moment I headed for the restroom.

"And once I saw Opal had picked up a gun, I took it from her in the event she was accidentally about to squeeze the trigger, and that's the end of it. Shep came out and asked me to put the gun down, and I did. I have no idea how this happened or why." The argument Perry was having earlier with that man in the hall before the show began runs through my mind.

"Okay, great," she says. "I'll need your full name and address and, of course, we'll have to run your prints."

"My prints?"

"Yes, your fingerprints." She tosses a quick glance to the woods. "We already have Opal's on file."

"Why does this not surprise me?" I say it low, but she chuckles regardless.

"I guess you know Opal well enough. Name and address, please."

Oh God. If ever I wanted to kill my ex twice over, it's right about now.

"Bowie." I swallow hard. "Buxom." I gasp. "I'm sorry. Brighton. Gah! I mean, Bixby, um, *Binx*." Oh dear Lord up in heaven. I might just ring my Uncle Vinnie's neck, too. "Bowie Binx. Sorry—I'm a bit nervous."

"Don't be." She waves it off. "You just saw a dead body. And you picked up a gun. Two things that can put the jitters in just about anyone. Address, please."

I offer a pleading look to Shep and my stomach ignites with heat. My hormones have never been good at unleashing themselves at an appropriate moment.

Shep gives a long blink of disdain before looking her way.

"Bowie is staying with me, in my spare cabin," he says it with a sigh.

The woman lifts a curious brow, first at him, then at me. She pulls her phone forward before looking to Shep.

"So, how exactly do the two of you know each other?" she poses the question my way, but Shep clears his throat, clearly wanting to take the wheel on the half-truth express.

"Opal introduced us." His lips rise with a tight smile. "Bowie is managing the café. Regina was let go of her position."

A soft chuckle emits from the woman.

"Well then." The words stream from her, rife with sarcasm, as she looks up and down at me.

And why do I suddenly feel as if she's judging me?

She leans in. "Let me reintroduce myself. Nora Grimsley. I'm one of Shepherd's many, many exes. If you feel the need to press charges or speak with me about the homicide at hand"—she holds out a business card—"feel free to call." She scowls at Shep before taking off.

I bite down over my lip a moment. "I take it things ended badly?"

Shep folds his arms across his chest. "They didn't end well, but it was for the best. Let's get you inside. You're shivering."

"Did you mean what you said? About the cabin?" I won't lie. The word *cabin* invokes images of a roaring fire, a cozy bed covered with a handmade quilt, and a stack of fresh made pancakes magically waiting for me in the morning. A girl can dream. I can just see myself swaddled in patchwork quilts. And what I wouldn't do to lose myself beneath the covers with this man—I mean, this man's cabin.

Shepherd tips his head to the right as he inspects me. "Yes, as a favor to Opal."

"Of course." My lips twist. "For Opal."

I head back into the manor where about a dozen cute furry kitties greet me and I pick up the one nearest to me, an exotic looking creature with dark stripes and spots against his tan fur.

The lights in the venue hall have raised another notch and the murmur of voices is deafening.

A blonde runs over holding the hand of a man with a scraggly beard, and I recognize her from earlier as Perry's girlfriend, Devin O'Malley.

"Oh, please tell me he's going to be all right." She gives my shoulders a quick shake. "Nicki said you were out there with him." Her lips are quivering, and her eyes glitter with tears.

"Um"—I hitch my thumb to the open door in the back—"I'm not really sure I'm qualified to say how he's doing."

He's doing *dead*, but I'm pretty sure it's not my place to break it to her.

The look of worry on her face is quickly replaced with anger.

"Come on, Bud," she snaps. "It's time we see this for ourselves." She yanks him away and I watch as they make their way out of the room. That must be her brother, the one she threw herself on earlier in the night. Something about the way Devin flipped her emotions on a dime doesn't sit well with me. I've seen every kind of grieving possible. Believe me, the mob can make an entire rainbow of grief happen and I've seen a rainbow of boo-hoos, too. I can spot bogus bereavement in a crowd any day, and I think I just did.

A shiver runs through me as I delve deeper into the crowded room and I gasp as I spot the man who was arguing with Perry just before the show. It's the one he got into a shoving match with.

He gives a quick look around the room. And as the sheriff's department begins to stream in, he streams right on out.

How do you like that? Well, I can't say I blame the guy. I don't plan on sticking around either.

Before long, the room clears out. Detective Grimsley lets me know she wants me to stop by the sheriff's department at some point tomorrow to take my prints. Nothing to worry about, procedure only.

Too bad for me, because I'm already worried about it.

Opal asks me to close the place down. Saying she needs her beauty sleep, she scoops up four cats and heads for the stairs.

Tilly and I herd the remainder of the people out of the hall and leave the sheriff's department to handle the rest of their business.

Soon, it's just Shepherd and me standing in front of the manor with a sky full of spring stars, the scent of murder still fresh in the air.

He gives me a ride to his place, no less than three city blocks from the manor, a welcome relief, considering the fact I could easily walk to work until I get Wanda fixed.

Shep lives on a tree-lined street, last house on the block in a cabin that looks as if it's made out of Lincoln Logs. He walks me around back and lets me into a cozy one-bedroom that's furnished with a comfy black and white checkered sofa and small round table up front, big enough for two. There's a fireplace and a braided rug, a coffee maker, and fridge. And oddly, that's about all I care about.

"How much do I owe you?" I hear the words streaming from my lips, and a part of me wants to shake my head.

"It's on Opal." He gives a little wink and my stomach is right back to bisecting with heat. His dark hair looks thick and glossy, and my fingers fight the urge to run through it. "Are you going to be okay?"

"Yeah, sure." Good to know this new version of me doesn't seem to have a problem with fibbing.

"I'm sorry you had such a rough night." He takes a breath and his chest expands to the width of the door. "Regardless, welcome to Starry Falls."

"Thank you."

He says goodnight, and I lock the door behind him.

I've been in this crazy town for less than twenty-four hours and I've already gained employment, found a murder victim, became a suspect, and met a man with the most amazing eyes I've ever seen.

Something buzzes in my pocket and I jump as I pull out that burner phone Uncle Vinnie gave me. I stare at the device as if it were a portal to another world entirely, one I never want to return to, not that I can.

A part of me hesitates to answer it and I let it ring endlessly in my hand until it finally goes quiet.

I'm too tired, too beat down, too weary right down to my soul to go there tonight.

Instead, I crawl into the most comfortable bed in the world and curl up with about a dozen patchwork quilts and dream of Perry Flint's lifeless body staring up at the sky.

Somebody killed Perry Flint tonight, and they just might get away with murder.

5

The café at the manor is bustling this morning with what I would classify as a bona fide rush. It's all hands on deck, working the floor, and the cooks in the back have already threatened to quit twice before ten in the morning before the crowd finally dies down.

Opal waltzes in wearing a lavender and black dress with puffy sleeves and black beading running down the front. She has on her signature red lipstick and her eyes are heavily drawn in with black kohl and dark eye shadow to boot. But her best accessory by far is the fuzzy cat in her arms that resembles a miniature leopard.

"Hello, cutie," I say, leaning over the counter and giving the sweet feline a quick scratch between the ears. Its eyes glow like ambers and it has a genuine inquisitiveness about it. "I do believe you were the first creature I met in this town."

Opal drops a kiss to its ear. "This is King. He's in charge of the manor. The rest of the cats are his minions." She gives a little wink before leaning in. "Who knew having a homicide on the grounds would be good for business?" Her eyes grow large a moment.

Tilly nods. "That's right. I think we easily made twice as much as we normally do by afternoon."

Opal's mouth rounds out with delight. "If I had any idea it would double my morning revenue, I'd order up a body or two more often." She belts out a laugh before looking to Tilly. "Don't forget about Stitch Witchery tonight. I'll need the library arranged in preparation." She taps her fingertips together. "And ask the chef to whip up some scones. No raisins this time." She wrinkles her nose as Tilly glides a cup of coffee her way and she takes off to greet the customers.

"Stitch Witchery?" I raise a brow at Tilly.

She's got her hair up in a messy bun and there's a bit of a cinnamon roll swirly effect going on with those chunky highlights of hers. She's squeezed herself into a tube top that I'm not one hundred percent certain meets the dress code

I'm about to implement, but since I can't afford to send anyone home to change, least of all her, I decide to let it slide for today. And if I'm being completely honest, Tilly's lack of proper accouterments might just be a contributing factor to the mostly male masses that have poured through the door.

"It's a stitch and bitch." Tilly pours herself a cup of coffee. "But since we're not allowed to use what Opal likes to call salty language, she's sort of given it a name she can live with. It's another ploy of hers to milk money from the masses. In the event you haven't noticed, Opal is a displaced socialite trying to claw her way up from the ashes."

"That's right. You mentioned the baton girl and the feds." I shake my head at the thought. I'm feeling more and more solidarity with the woman by the hour. I glance her way and note she's donned a pair of fishnet stockings that have rhinestones riding up the back of the seam. It takes a lot of character to get away with wearing something like that this early in the morning. "I like her." I shrug. "She's eccentric and completely out of touch with the common people. I've been disillusioned a time or two myself. I have a feeling we'll get along just fine."

Tilly bats her lashes my way as if she were innocent. But judging by the sarcastic look in her eyes, she's got a zinger she's ready to fire away.

"Did you and Shep get along just fine last night?"

And there it is.

"What? No." My cheeks heat ten degrees. "Not that I would have minded if we did, but he didn't throw out the offer. I don't think he cares for me. He was a little curt if you ask me."

"That's his MO. I wish I could say he's a teddy bear once you get to know him, but I don't think too many people ever really get to know him." Her mouth falls open as she hitches her head toward the door. "Speak of the devil."

"Morning, ladies." He offers a quick nod. "The usual," he says to Tilly as he heads off for a window seat and unpacks a laptop from his briefcase.

She pours a cup of coffee, black, and glides it my way.

"By all means, do the honors," she says as a small group wanders in. "I'll take over the counter."

Not one to look a gift horse in the mouth, or a ten-minute break, I whisk the coffee off to the grump near the window and take a seat across from him.

"Whatcha working on?" I try to lean forward and see the screen, but he moves the laptop over an inch, obstructing my view.

"You left this morning." He takes a careful sip of his coffee before landing it on the table once again.

His dark hair is slicked back, his eyes look icy in that sexy sled dog way, and every female in a ten-table radius is at full attention.

"I didn't know I was required to stay." I flash a short-lived smile. "I saw how close we were to the manor and I needed to open. I didn't want to bother you for a lift, so I walked. Your turn. What are you, an attorney or something?" I lift a finger to the laptop.

"Author. I write under the name S. J. Wexler."

I suck in a quick breath. "As in *the* S. J. Wexler? Thriller author?"

"Yes." A smile teases on his lips, but he's too stubborn to give it. But I can see the pride dancing in his eyes and a part of me wants to call him on it. "Have you read any of my books?"

"No, but I see them all over. My father was actually a big thriller fan." I choose not to let him in on the fact my father was starring in a thriller of his own. Spoiler alert: it's not ending well for him. "So you're kind of famous." I'm suddenly starstruck by this beautiful man. A man with a hot face is a dime a dozen. But a man with a hot face and a hot mind is a needle in a jerk stack for lack of a better euphemism. "No wonder all the girls can't help but stare. I mean, they're staring for far more obvious reasons as well, but I get the feeling you're aware of that, too."

He tips his head back as he takes me in.

"Strong, silent type. I like that," I say as my body heat spikes. "Well, I'd best leave before my deodorant expires, and considering that I don't have on any, that could pose a deadly threat to us both. But thank you for the room and shower. I really appreciate that. Hey? Can I come back tonight?"

He dips his chin and looks up at me an inordinate amount of time.

"Yes. On Opal's insistence." He frowns as he adds that little tidbit. "I'll be sure to leave an ample tip for you so you can stop off at the store and stock up on your hygiene needs."

"Oh, right." My underarms bite with heat once again as if they know the hygienic spotlight is being pointed right at them. "So tell me something about yourself. Were you born and raised in Starry Falls? Have you always been a writer? I know for a fact you were engaged to the Grim Reaper I met last night." Tilly gave me the lowdown when she got here. Okay, so I may have shaken it out of her. But I couldn't help it. I like to keep tabs on the people in my life. It's in my blood to be in the know.

His lips curl when I refer to his ex as the Grim Reaper.

"Hey?" I beam with pride of my own. "I think I almost got a smile out of you."

"You'll have to work harder."

I nod. "Believe me, I get it. Anyone who wants a single thing out of me is going to have to work pretty darn hard themselves. So you got burned on the relation*shep* front, huh? Is that what this whole wall of steel is about?" I take a sip from his coffee and his eyes widen in horror.

"Oh, right. Sorry." I glide the mug back in his direction. "So Starry Falls? Born and raised?"

"Maple Grove, a few towns over." He strums his fingers over the table. "I landed in Starry Falls about two years ago. It's nice. The people are nice. They leave me alone."

"Is that like a hint?" I squint over at him a moment too long. "Never mind. I told you a little about my dad. What about your family?" I can't stop looking at his hypnotizing eyes. No wonder he wants to be left alone. His face can't help but cast a spell over people.

He leans in just a notch, his lips curling at the edges once again.

"My father is in prison," he whispers.

"No kidding?" I spike in my seat. "So is mine!" Okay, so it's nothing to get overly excited about, but let's face it, that's common ground you simply don't get to have with a whole lot of people.

He leans in, that same bored look on his face is unflinching. "Did he kill your stepmother?"

I gasp at the thought. "Geez. No. That's brutal. So that's why you've got this whole tough guy persona going on? You were raised by wolves."

He gives a long blink. "You're not that far off. But my mother was decent. Still is. So are my brother and sister."

My mouth falls open with surprise. "*I* have a brother and a sister." I lean in. "Any marriages? Children?"

"Nope, and not that I know of."

"Ha-ha, I get it. I hear you get around. I'd stay off the DNA websites if I were you." And if I were me, too, for entirely different reasons.

A laugh bubbles from me, but his flat expression doesn't waver.

"So what's the new story about?" I peer over at the laptop, and this time he doesn't seem to mind me catching a glimpse, not that I can make heads or tails from all the errant letters running around the page.

"It's about a mystery woman who stumbles into town, and then just as quickly stumbles upon a body. I'll give you a hint. I think she's somehow involved."

I sober up real quick and shoot him the stink eye. But before I can let a smart-aleck comment fly, a shadow darkens the table and I look up to see Detective Grimsley frowning down at the two of us.

"We're ready for your close-up, Ms. Binx."

6

Dead.

I'd rather be dead.

I feel as if I've died and gone somewhere, but just not heaven, and maybe not quite hell either.

Detective Grimsley, Nora, who actually asked me twice not to call her by her first name, was insistent that we head down to Woodley County. And in an odd turn of events, Shepherd Wexler, author extraordinaire and professional scowler, offered to give me a ride himself. Seeing that it was either him or her in the glorified paddy wagon, I hopped shotgun in his truck. Little did I know that all the way to Woodley—a whopping twenty-minute drive—he would be not-so-gently interrogating me about my family, the brother and sister I inadvertently brought up, and that father of mine who is doing time and why. About halfway there, I finally figured out I hopped into the wrong car.

The Woodley County Sheriff's Department is gray and dismal, and despite the fact it's a warm spring day, everyone inside is huddled in sweaters and jackets because it's a frosty minus ten degrees in here. I'm still stuck in my jogging clothes, and I'm guessing sooner or later someone is going to notice—mostly due to the ripe scent I'll be emitting, and they'll be forced to run me out of town.

Nora walks us to the back, and before I know it, I've filled out all the vital information via the phony records my Uncle Vinnie furnished me with. Fake name. Fake Social Security number. Let's hope to God the real owner of those dicey digits isn't wanted for a major felony, or I'll have a little more in common with my father than I bargained for.

Nora drags me into her office and conducts another quickie interview about the things I witnessed last night. After I fill her in once again on the things that happened, she excuses herself briefly and steps outside to talk to Shep.

The two of them murmur between themselves while I'm left to my own devices, so I do the only thing I can do—snoop. A couple of pictures are lined up on the shelf behind her desk, and surprisingly, not one of them stars her former beau. There's a lip balm and a compact lying loose on the edge of her desk and a smattering of paperwork strewn over it.

A file marked *Flint* in large red letters sits less than a foot from me, and as much as I'd like to mind my own business, I reach over and flip it open. I'm not too worried about getting busted due to the arctic blast coming from the AC unit at seventy miles per hour. I don't think it would be a far cry to blame it on the hurricane force gale whipping through the office.

A yellow piece of paper stares back at me and my name is at the top of the list. Under it I see the name Opal Mortimer. Figures, we're both suspects. Both innocent, too, but I'm betting that doesn't carry much weight anymore. It's all about numbers and quotas, and putting innocent people away isn't all that big of a deal anymore.

I spot Shep's name at the bottom of the list, but he's the only one who's already had a line drawn through it. Figures. He's probably too good in bed to get rid of. He's basically an asset to her. And if she's still interested in him, she might see me as a threat. I already mentioned that I stayed at his cabin last night. I needed an address, and God knows that Chicago, Connecticut baloney wasn't going to fly twice in a lifetime.

I glance to the list once again. Devin O'Malley, Richard Broadman, Nicki Magnolia.

Huh. Devin was Perry Flint's girlfriend. Richard was the hot-to-trot silver fox slash manager. And Nicki was Perry's assistant. But she doesn't have the name of the guy Perry got in a fight with just before he went on stage—most likely because she has no idea he exists.

Maybe I should say something?

But then, if I say something, I might garner more of her unwanted attention, and I'm already sweating like a pig just before a luau.

No thank you. I've got places to go and people to see, *outside* of the prison system. It's probably best I let her do her job. But then again, if she doesn't make an arrest soon, she just might come sniffing back my way, or in Opal's direction. And for knowing someone for less than twenty-four hours, I sure seem to have built up an affection for the crazy broad.

Nope, we're not going down.

And I'll do whatever I can to stop it from happening.

Nora knocks on the door and I startle, jumping to my feet and bolting from her office.

She lifts her chin my way, and I can't help but note she has a hardened look about her. She would have made an excellent mobster. Her dark lipstick and heavy angry eyes let me know she's not interested in entertaining niceties with me—or perhaps anybody else sucking up oxygen at the moment.

"Don't leave town," she says it like a threat and my mouth falls open, because as soon as I have enough to resurrect Wanda from the dead, I plan on doing just that.

"Okay," I hear myself say.

I know for a fact there's nothing they can do if I skip.

It's not like I'm under arrest.

"Good." She pulls her lips in a line. "Because if you do, I'll hunt you down and arrest you." Her dark eyes hook to Shep's. "It was nice seeing you again. Do you have any book signings coming up?"

His shoulders twitch. "One in town."

She gives a little laugh. "Lucky for you, that's the only place you're allowed to be. No out-of-state trips. Hopefully, we'll have this wrapped up in a few days." She lifts her gaze to me. "Quicker if we get a confession."

Shep thanks her and navigates us the heck out of there.

"Hey?" I look back at the building he just hustled us out of. "Why do I get the feeling she thinks I pulled the trigger?"

"Maybe because you were left holding the murder weapon."

"You think you're funny, don't you?" A glittering sign that reads *half off all clearance* catches my eye from across the street. "Whoa." I pull us to a stop while checking the place out. "I'm just a smidge excited about that sale, but the just a smidge part is literal because it's a secondhand store. Normally, I wouldn't pay it any mind, but at the moment I'm down one wardrobe." I dig into my pocket for the tips I shoved in it this morning and count out nine dollars and thirty-seven cents, mostly in quarters. "You wouldn't mind if I ran in, would you? I'll take less than ten minutes. I could really use another pair of everything."

"Knock yourself out. I don't mind ducking in and checking out the book section. I'm a bit of a collector." He digs into his pocket and lands a bill in my hand before closing my fingers. "I meant to tip you before we left the café."

"Smooth, Wexler. Real smooth."

We get into the thrift shop and I wait until he disappears for the book section before checking out what he gave me and I gasp at the sight of it. With one zero it would have been too much, but with two it's an abundance of riches.

"A hundred dollars," I whisper to myself. A part of me says hunt him down and give it back, but the part of me who's itching for something a little less encrusted to wear says make smart choices in the clearance aisle, and I do just that.

After almost an hour, I call it a success and ante up. Shep meets me at the front and helps me with my bags as we load up the back of his truck.

"Would you look at this?" I wiggle my greatest find in his face as we head back toward Starry Falls.

"What's that?" He pulls back and inspects it a moment. "Dead cow?"

"That's right. But it's not just any dead cow. It's a certified Louis Vuitton *Neverfull* dead cow. I'm guessing it's about eighteen years old judging by the oil stains on the shoulder straps and the small hole on the piping. But it's new to me, and you better believe I'm going to take care of this baby as if I pushed it from my loins."

"Good. I'm glad you found something that gives you joy."

"You and me both. What about you? Find any good books to read?" I'd point out that he came out empty-handed, but that might spoil the fun.

"Found three of my own in there." He shrugs. "A few others I thought were interesting but didn't pull the trigger."

"I guess you don't have much time to read since you're always writing your own stuff. I hear writing's a lonely profession. You ever think about getting a pet?" I suck in a quick breath. "Hey, we should get a dog!"

"*We?*" He sounds mildly panicked.

"Yeah, you know, back at the cabin."

"You may not realize this yet, but Starry Falls is a feline kind of town."

"Oh, right. I forgot about King and his minions. In that case, let's just snatch one of them flirty felines up. You know what they say about cats. Once you feed them, they'll never want to leave."

He frowns my way. "You're not part feline, are you?"

"Very funny."

We pull into the driveway next to his cabin and I quickly scoop up my haul.

"Shep, thank you for all this." I hoist the bags into my arms as I look him in the eye.

A smile flickers on his lips, and if I blinked, I would have missed it.

"You're welcome, Bowie. Can I ask what your dad went to prison for?"

My mouth opens and I can't seem to draw a single lie out of it.

"Let's just say he made the government very, very angry."

He gives a quick nod. "I get it."

I shrug up at him. "I wish I did."

His eyes search mine and I resist the urge to give the dark scruff on his cheeks a playful scratch.

Before I can say goodbye or run for my life, that warm, fuzzy feeling takes over and an electrical current courses through me. The world around me seems to close off and in my mind's eye, I see Shep standing in a room filled with books. He's speaking to a crowd when a woman bulldozes her way through the crowd, wraps her hands around his neck, and begins to throttle him.

"Bowie?" The sound of his voice forces me to take a sharp breath. "Are you okay?"

"I'm fine." I give several hard blinks as the world rushes back to life around me. "Hey? Um, you mentioned that you had an author signing coming up here in Starry Falls?"

"This Thursday at the Book Basement right on Main Street. Seven-thirty. You're more than welcome to come."

"I wouldn't miss it."

His eyes press to mine a moment before he nods, and we part ways.

I'll be there, all right.

Some loon is about to do her best to snuff the life out of him, and I'm going to do my best to stop her.

But first, I need to get Detective Grimsley to draw a line through my name—and Opal's, too.

7

The Mortimer Manor sits like a stone in the path of this otherwise cheery and sunny day, or at least what's left of it. The café is lit a little too bright and the scent of French fries, onion rings, and hamburgers lingers in the air.

King sits on Opal's lap with his tail gently whipping her on the chin while Tilly and I catch a breather from the early dinner rush that just blew through the place.

"Did you know half the people I served asked me what the special was?" I direct it to Opal, but Tilly is the one that scoffs.

"Good idea. We should have a special. How about dead man stew? Half the people I served wanted a firsthand account of how I found Perry Flint."

"You didn't find Perry Flint," I'm quick to inform her.

"Yeah"—she wrinkles her nose—"but they don't know that."

A couple of the waitresses, Thea and Flo, head this way. I'd say they were both in their early twenties. Thea has reddish-brown hair, long and glossy. Her face is covered with a healthy dusting of freckles, and she has a white picket fence smile for just about everyone she greets.

And for as sunny as Thea can be, Flo is just that dark. She's basically a Goth girl with black harshly dyed hair and eyebrows that I think are tattooed onto her forehead in the shape of sharp pointy peaks. Her perpetual frown is painted black, and she has that overall look in her eyes that says *I just might kill you in your sleep*.

She grunts my way, "The place is empty. What do we do now?"

"I know." Opal gives a silent clap. "Bash men."

Tilly clucks her tongue. "If we bash men now, what will we do at the Stitch and Witch?"

"Stitch Witchery," Opal corrects as she gives King a quick stroke over his pleasantly spotted back. "And you're so right."

"We can think of a monthly special," I say just as the bell on the door chimes and in strides a familiar face.

It's Nicki Magnolia.

"Nicki," I say as I head her way. After my little thrift shop adventure, I did a quick change before coming back to the café, and now I'm feeling cute in my skinny jeans and blue-checkered top. My mother would say I looked like a country bumpkin, but I'd rather look like anything that belonged in the country than something that belonged in a women's correctional facility. "How can I help you? Would you like a table or a booth?"

Tilly and Opal swarm around me as we await her answer.

"Neither." She makes a face. Her dark hair is pulled back tight into a bun, and she's dressed as if she's off to corporate America in a navy blouse and matching skirt. "I was told by the sheriff's department that I could pick up any of Perry's things they didn't take."

"Oh, sure." Tilly waves for her to follow and both Opal and I tag along as well.

Tilly leads us out of the café and through the maroon carpeted hall where hordes of cats lounge on their bloated bellies. I scoop up a tan furry cat that looks like a miniature bear with an adorably smushed face, and already I've decided to try my best to lure this sweet thing back to the cabin. I give a quick glance down south and note she's a she.

Opal leans in. "That's Molly and I can tell by that gleam in your eye you're quietly staging a catnapping. You'll have to try harder. Molly is one of my prized possessions."

I make a face at the older and somehow significantly *wiser* woman.

"You're intuitive," I say. "Oh, I almost forgot." I lean her way and whisper, "I had another spell." I tick my head as if that would aid in alluding to what I meant to say. "I'll tell you about it later."

"*Ooh!*" She gives an enthusiastic clap just as we arrive at the back room where Perry had set his things before heading on stage. It's a small space with nothing more than the table and a few chairs. There's a fake ficus in the corner, an attached bathroom, and a water cooler. A green room of sorts for whoever is about to take the stage.

"Thank you," Nicki says with marked relief as she picks up a backpack off the table in the middle of the room. "I was actually worried someone would break in here and try to steal Perry's memorabilia. You know, it goes up in value considerably once someone like Perry passes away."

Tilly nods her way. "And I bet it skyrockets once a homicide takes place. You know, it gives it that whole creep factor."

Nicki looks as if she's about to be sick. "I guess I didn't think of that."

Opal groans, "How I wish I would have thought about killing my ex. He was in prison for taking advantage of the IRS, or was it the government?" She taps a finger to her chin. "Or maybe it was both?"

"Nicki"—I step in—"you have my condolences. What are you going to do now? You know, for work?"

"I haven't thought that far ahead. I have some money saved up. I think I'll need a minute to get my head together."

"Good plan," I say. "Did you and Perry get along for the most part? I mean, you were his personal assistant. He was probably the most comfortable with you, so you saw him at his worst. That could be tough on any relationship."

"I did see him at his worst." She glances to the ceiling. "And I guess he saw me at my worst, too. We were practically inseparable."

Tilly juts her head forward. "I'm guessing his girlfriend didn't really like that. Another woman in close proximity.

You're a pretty girl. He was a good-looking guy. You ever knock boots with the country crooner? You can tell us. It won't leave this room."

Nicki belts out a soft laugh. "No, actually, that never happened." Her cheeks ignite into pink flares. "But if I'm being truthful, it did cross my mind. He was with Devin, though." Her jaw clenches a moment. "Don't get me wrong. Devin is pretty, and fun, and flirty, but I never thought she deserved him." She begins to head for the door and I casually block her path.

"Why is that?" I ask, trying not to sound too hostile. A part of me wants to shake the girl because she just might hold the key between me and an orange jumpsuit that's to be worn in and out of season.

Her shoulders lift to her ears. "Have you ever just had a feeling about someone?"

"Yes," I say a little too quickly. But what I won't tell her is that I usually get that feeling when it's far too late. If only I had that feeling about Johnny Rizzo about two years ago, I wouldn't be wearing secondhand clothes in a glorified litter box while starring as a murder suspect in my very own nightmare. Not that the manor is a glorified litter box, but it fit the description and at the moment I needed a good sarcastic moniker for this place. A thought comes to me.

"Hey, Nicki? Where can I find Devin? She took off her earrings earlier in the night while we were talking. She said they were too heavy. Anyway, she set them down and walked away. I'd really like to give them back."

She rolls her eyes. "That's Devin in a nutshell." She glances to the floor a moment. "She doesn't really work, unless you call spending all of Perry's money a job. She hangs out at a country western bar down in Scooter Springs called the Tumbleweed Tavern a lot. She's forever talking about it. She even tried to get me to go once, but I told her I didn't mix business with pleasure." A small laugh evicts from her. "Truth is, I couldn't stand to see her slobber all over Perry. I was embarrassed for the both of them." She hikes her backpack up a notch. "Thanks, ladies. I'll show myself out."

Tilly gives a little hop on her feet as she looks my way. "Are you thinking what I'm thinking?"

Opal lifts a brow with her crimson lips swimming with glee. "Yes. We'll spike the monthly special with whiskey and garner twice the tips. I'll take ten percent off the top since I came up with the idea, of course."

Why do I get the feeling in six months' time, I'll be wishing I had a *feeling* about Opal Mortimer?

I shake my head at her. "We head over to the Tumbleweed Tavern."

Opal gives a solid blink. "Only if they have whiskey."

I press a quick kiss to Molly's furry forehead. "It looks as if we're about to two-step our way to a suspect, and just maybe the killer."

8

It turns out, Scooter Springs is only twenty minutes away from Starry falls, but it took us forty due to the fact we needed to feed every feline in the state of Vermont. But once we flew into town—and I do mean flew, considering Tilly drove as if all four tires were on fire—we arrived at our destination no worse for wear and about fifty pounds lighter once we dumped all that kitty kibble.

The Tumbleweed Tavern is more or less a theme restaurant slash bar with wooden shutters for doors and sawdust on the floor, country music twanging at top volume, and bodies swiftly moving in a choreographed rhythm across a plywood dance floor. It's hot and sweaty and the scent of cheap booze and hot wings permeates the place.

Opal has donned a long, black, glittery number with a pair of hot pink leggings underneath it. Nice to know she's as fearless in fashion as she is with her liver. She's been nipping off a sterling silver flask ever since we left and her breath is enough to inebriate everyone in this tawdry tavern.

Tilly squeals as she takes the place in—excited for all the untapped coital potential, no doubt. Tilly has donned a skirt so short I'm too embarrassed to look at the hemline, and her top is more of a concept than a reality, but I'm not one to talk. I may or may not have pulled out a slinky red dress out of my thrift store haul I scored this afternoon. It's adorable and sexy all at the same time, has an edginess about it typically only found in Christmas tinsel, and if all goes well, by the end of the night, I just might want to marry it.

Tilly bumps her hip to mine. "Fingerprinted in the afternoon, taking a bite out of crime and hunky men in the evening."

"That's worrisome." I swat the air between us. "Speaking of things that are worrisome, I had another *preview*." I say *preview* in air quotes. To be honest, I've never liked calling them visions. It makes me sound as if I've gone pro. I consider myself more of an accidental voyeur as far as future events are concerned, and due to my more than dicey track record, I have no business paying attention to my futuristic musings, let alone verbalizing them for others.

Tilly gasps as she grabs onto Opal.

"Tell us," she demands as we step out of the line of traffic streaming in.

"Okay, Shep told me he's having a book signing this Thursday. And no sooner did he mention it than I saw a blonde attacking him at the signing and wrapping her hands around his neck."

Opal grunts as if she were shot. "Oh dear heavens, we've got a serial killer on the loose and she's about to strike down our Shepherd."

"I don't know." I shrug. "Newsflash: I'm not always right."

Opal's eyes enlarge. "You were right about *me*—sort of."

"And in those last two words lies the caveat," I say. "My prediction was wildly misconstrued."

Tilly presses her watery blue eyes into mine. "Bowie, how do you have this ability? Were you electrocuted as a child? Cursed by a powerful witch? Did you kick a dog in the cookies?"

Opal groans, "Hurting an animal would really tick off the universe."

"Well, I didn't kick a dog in the cookies, but I'm not so sure about that ticking off the universe part. My grandmother and sister have this—thing. It actually has a name. It's called transmundane, and I fall under the umbrella of something called sibylline. From what I understand, there are other supernatural abilities, too. Some can read minds; others can see the dead—"

"What?" Tilly squawks. "Hey, I want that one. I want to see the dead!"

Opal clutches at that cuff of baubles around her neck. "I saw the dead a couple of days ago and, believe me, it's not all it's cracked up to be."

Tilly swats her on the arm. "She's talking ghosts."

"*Ooh.*" Opal taps the tips of her fingers together in a show of excitement. "Trade your gift in, Bowie, and get that one. I'm positive the manor is haunted. I'd like for you to confirm it for me. I've heard rumors of a haunted B&B down in Honey Hollow and they're making a killing off tourists. Pardon the pun. That would be a wonderful revenue maker for me. You can't always think of yourself, you know. See about getting a refund for that psychic gone wrong gig. Or maybe there's an exchange program you can look into?"

My mouth hangs open.

"Ugh," Tilly moans at something over my shoulder. "Jessie's here, showing off the turquoise cowboy boots I picked up in Nashville last summer. And is that my ex she's dancing with?" She zips off to scold her teen gone wild while Opal and I plop down at the bar.

I don't see a single sign of Devin and I'm beginning to wonder if my time would have been better spent trying to lure Molly the teddy bear cat out to the cabin with me. I could have taken off a few layers of clothing... knocked on Shep's door...

"Earth to David Bowie." Opal knocks her shoulder to mine as she quickly navigates us to the bar. "Bartender, two whiskey sours, please."

I'm quick to shake my head. "Oh, I don't drink."

"You do if you want to work for me," she drones it out in that socialite accent I've come to adore.

"Are you kidding?" I balk at the thought of lighting up my liver. "That brown liquid is tantamount to truth serum." And Lord knows there are some truths nobody should know about. Not to mention my sibylline superpowers tend to go haywire if I have too much caffeine or alcohol. My mind has been known to go on lockdown for eight hours of defective divination. "So tell me, Opal, what's going on with the manor?"

"Oh, it's a heap of junk. The only thing my husband left me with. Sure, he said it's mine free and clear, but I still have to come up with the taxes for the place." The bartender slides the drinks our way and Opal scoops them both up for herself. "And I've yet to live the way as to which I'm accustomed. If only there was a way to bilk the residents of Starry Falls for all they're worth."

"I take it you're not from Starry Falls?"

She lifts her whiskey sour as if to toast me. "Sterling Lake born and bred. About an hour's drive from Starry Falls." She makes a face. "Starry Falls may as well be a third-world country compared to Sterling—land where the champagne flows freely and the foie gras is served breakfast, lunch, and dinner." She gives a wistful shake of the head. "I'd give anything to have a reversal of fortune."

"How about fifty percent?"

She gives me the side-eye. "For what?"

"For me to triple your profit at the manor with a few minor changes."

"Fifteen, final offer."

"I'll take it." I hold out my hand and she shakes it. The way I look at it, it's fifteen percent more than I had to begin with. Besides, I see lots of *legal* potential in that old place. I hope.

"So what's your proper name, Bowie Binx? Bowden? Bowella? Bobo, perhaps?" She takes a sip of her drink.

"Just Bowie. We're not really fancy people down in—"

"Chicago, Connecticut." She waves me off. "Shepherd filled me in." She leans my way. "And I'm fully aware it's a cover. You might have the good detective fooled, but you can't pull the wool sweater over this old biddy's peepers."

I clamp my lips shut. She might have pinned the tail on this fugitive donkey, but I'm not taking the bait.

Speaking of the good detective, I'm about to ask her a few innocuous questions about Nora Grimsley when I spot the hot-to-trot blonde that dragged me out to this boot scootin' establishment to begin with.

"I see Devin O'Malley at six o'clock. It looks like it's go time, Opal."

"Oh good." She glances over her shoulder. "I'll stay here and make sure the bartender is safe. Try not to get yourself killed."

"You bet."

Devin has her hair up in a waterfall of curls. She's donned a short denim skirt and is wearing a blue and white checkered top that's tied off just above her belly button, and

I can't help but note that's essentially what I was wearing earlier. If it wasn't for my longing to wear something sultry, we could have been twins. I pull my red dress down a notch and head her way.

Devin is already two-stepping with the best of them, with her hands on her hips, her whole body rocking with the motion. She's standing in a long line of people as they rock back and forth, so I cut right in front of her and go with the rockin' flow.

"Hey? I think I'm getting the hang of it," I shout up above the music at her and she laughs.

"No, you're actually not." She grabs ahold of my hips and tweaks them until I'm swinging in the other direction. "It's called the Sugar Shuffle. Now put some sugar into it. Move that body like you mean it."

I do as I'm told, and soon she's moving with a fire of her own right in front of me. The song mercifully comes to a conclusion, and I take a cue from her and clap with my hands high above my head as if a rock deity just stepped into the room.

Her eyes square over mine. "Don't I know you?"

I squint over at her a moment before slapping my thigh. "Starry Falls. We met before Perry Flint took the stage."

She cringes and I gasp as if it just dawned on me what it means.

"I'm so sorry." I gently place my hand over her shoulder as I offer my condolences. "How are you doing?"

A man pops up next to her, holding out a bottle of beer her way. That red hair, those heavily carved crow's feet, that scraggly beard—I recognize him, too.

"You're the brother, right?" I point his way.

Devin snatches the beer from his hands. "Bud, why don't you get another? This is for my friend." She winks my way as she hands it over and Bud takes off like a dutiful retriever. "I'm doing as well as can be expected. My brother didn't think it would do me any good to stay home and wallow, so here I am. What's your name again?" She takes a quick swig, keeping one eye on me at all times.

"Bowie. Bowie Binx. I work down at the Mortimer Manor."

"Sorry right back at you." She shudders before taking a much longer hit off her bottle.

"Nicki came by this afternoon." I try to connect my gaze to hers. "She picked up the rest of Perry's things in case you were wondering what happened to them."

"Oh good." She gives a quick blink. "I've got half my stuff at his place. The sheriff's department had it off limits. I don't know what they could have been looking for. Perry was a good guy. On the up and up." She pauses as if she caught herself in a lie. "Everyone knew that—everyone but Richard Broadman."

"*Richard*? Oh, the manager? I met him, too. Good-looking silver fox? My friend was hitting on him."

She rolls her eyes. "She probably got lucky, too. He's got a wife, but he won't let anyone know about her. Poor thing. Richard's a cheat through and through."

"Oh? So he was cheating Perry? You know, in a managerial sort of way?"

She gives a hard nod. "And, of course, Richard being Richard had to try to turn it around. He was always accusing Perry of getting in on something and not giving him his cut. Those two never got along, and I'll be honest, I'm not all that surprised with how things ended."

"With murder?"

She tips her amber bottle my way. "You said it, not me."

A couple strides in and I do a double take in their direction. It's none other than Shepherd Wexler with that brunette bombshell by his side, Regina something or other, and I can't help but frown at the way she's pawing all over him. Good for Opal for tossing the screaming banshee from the café.

Too bad there's not a way to toss her out of Starry Falls. Back in New Jersey it could have been done.

Shepherd scans the room and his eyes widen once he hits me. Suffice it to say, he doesn't look impressed, more like distressed—or more to the point, angry.

Why do I get the feeling I'm in trouble?

Devin glances to the bar. "I'd better find Bud. He has a way of lingering around the ladies, if you know what I mean."

She takes off, and in her place materialize Shep and Regina. Shep looks dangerous in a pair of jeans and a flannel. Regina looks like hell on heels in a white dress that looks as if it were sculpted onto her body.

"Hey?" She points her finger at my midsection. "I used to own a dress just like that." She leans in a notch, scrutinizing my bustline. "What do you know, that *is* mine. I took the buttons off the neckline to open it up. You're welcome." She snarls my way before looking to Shep. "The things you did to me in that dress." Her fingers walk up his chest as if they had a right to. "You just couldn't wait to take it off."

"That's funny," I mutter. "I'm suddenly feeling the same way."

Just the thought of Shep doing things to Regina in this dress makes me want to gag myself with a pitchfork.

"I think I'm going to have a nice little fire when I get home." I'm pretty sure the manmade materials this demented dress is made from will set off all kinds of noxious fumes. If the visual of Shep undressing Regina doesn't land me in the ER, the toxins seeping into my lungs will.

Wait a minute. Why would I care what Shep does with who, while she's wearing God knows what?

I catch him in a full scowl.

"Why are you looking at me like that?" I snap.

"Why are you here? And how did you arrive?" he snaps right back.

About ten different women swoon as soon as he barks my way. Something tells me they'd much rather prefer it if he barked their way, and come to think of it, so would I.

Shep's blue eyes siren out an icy shade of sexy, and that perennial scowl only seems to add to his wicked charm. He's by far the hottest man in this tumbleweed catastrophe, and probably all of Vermont if you want to get technical.

"Tilly gave me a ride," I confess. "Opal and I were just enjoying drinks at the bar. But since I chose not to imbibe, Opal is taking one for the team and downing my drink as well."

Regina looks to her right. "And since I do imbibe, I volunteer to help her do just that." She zooms off at the prospect of free liquor and Shep takes a full step closer to me. I can feel the warmth of his body, heating me like an inferno, and his spiced cologne just put my ovaries on high alert.

He leans in. "I saw you speaking to Devin O' Malley. You're here questioning a suspect, aren't you?"

"Why would I do that?"

"Because you want to clear your name."

"Don't forget about Opal." I cringe as I stuff my fingers into my mouth. "Okay, so what's it to you? I need that killer behind bars so I can get on with the rest of my life."

"Your life in Chicago, Connecticut?" He folds his arms across his chest and gets this know-it-all look in his eye.

I hold my breath a moment too long.

"Yes," I say. "Or, the one in Starry Falls. It's none of your business where I lay my head at night."

"It is if I'm your landlord."

"You're not my landlord. Are you?"

He gives a single nod.

"Okay, fine. I questioned Devin and I'm about to question Richard Broadman, too. And there's not a darn thing you can do to stop me."

"Bowie." He navigates us out of the dancing *line* of fire and his arm heats the right side of my body like a brushfire tearing its way through a pile of autumn leaves. "Somebody shot Perry Flint dead in cold blood. They've already killed once. There's no telling if they'll do it again. Believe me when I say, you don't want to try them. Leave this to the professionals."

A husky laugh rips through me. "No offense to your ex, but she's not my knight in shining armor. I've learned the hard way that sometimes in life you need to save yourself."

His cheek flinches and he looks unfairly handsome in the process.

"That sounds great for a greeting card, Bowie. But whoever killed Perry undoubtedly knows you were left holding the murder weapon. And once they figure out you're fishing around trying to throw your net around them, they're going to come after you." He dips his chin down a notch. "Do you want that?"

Shepherd Wexler has parts of me quivering that haven't quivered in a good long while. I'm tempted to nod and let him know I want whatever he's selling. He can take all the money I don't have. Heck, he can take the dress right off my back, seeing that he's an expert at it.

"No." I clear my throat. "I guess I don't want a killer coming after me." I can't help but glower over at him. "Don't you have a date to find? You'd better scoop her up before someone else decides to disrobe her."

He gives a long blink. "I'm not seeing Regina. She came by the cabin, and I told her I was going out."

"Oh? So she essentially invited herself?"

"Something like that."

My mouth rounds out. "So what were you going to do here?" I suck in a quick breath. "You were coming to investigate this case, weren't you? What happened to leaving it to the professionals?"

His lids hood a notch and all sorts of fireworks go off inside me.

"Bowie, I am a professional. Or at least I was. Up until six months ago, I was the lead homicide detective down at the Woodley Sheriff's Department."

"You were?" My mouth falls open with delight. "Why'd they fire you?"

He frowns hard. "Nobody fired me. I retired early."

"Oh, I guess that writing gig is working out pretty well for you then."

"Something like that. Anyway, this is not for you. Steer clear, got it?"

Devin spins her way back to the dance floor, and no sooner does she catch my eye than I get that old familiar tunnel vision. A warm feeling washes over my body, and in my mind's eye, I see Devin looking right at me, panting, her hair and clothes disheveled. *"Okay, fine,"* she shouts. *"You caught me. I'm guilty. Are you happy? Perry left me no choice. I had to do it. He forced my hand. And you're not going to tell anyone, you hear me?"*

"Bowie?" Shep leans in. "Do us both a favor and steer clear of this case."

I wobble on my feet, and he wraps his hand around my waist.

"Whoa." His warm breath caresses my cheek. "Easy there. Let's get some coffee in you."

"Sounds like a plan," I say as we pass Devin up and head for the bar.

It looks as if I'll be steering clear of the case soon enough.

Just as soon as they arrest Devin O'Malley.

She's the killer, and I just had the vision to prove it.

Shep offers to drive Opal and me back to Starry Falls. Tilly and Regina each found a partner to spin them round and round.

No sooner do I get settled in my cabin than I hear a muffled ringing sound coming from the cookie jar on the kitchen counter, and I freeze solid for a moment because that just so happens to be where I hid that burner phone Uncle Vinnie gave me.

I speed over and pull it out, jumping on the balls of my feet to hear my sweet Uncle Vinnie's voice.

"Hello!" I trill. "I miss you so much! I just can't wait to tell you all about my crazy adventure. First of all—"

"Stella? Shut up, Stella! This is Johnny. Where the hell are you? We gotta talk."

It's Johnny.

I hold the phone out as if it just morphed into a viper. I have to get rid of it. I can't have Johnny tracking me down. I don't want to speak to him ever again.

My feet traipse over to the bathroom and I drop the phone into the toilet as Johnny screams my name, and then I flush.

My heart jackhammers against my chest as I watch the phone go down.

If only it could take my past along with it.

9

The entire next day I'm shaken to the core. I somehow managed to muddle through the morning rush, the lunch rush, and the stragglers who showed up for dinner.

I also managed to avoid any undue contact with Shepherd Wexler. He came in about ten in the morning and set up shop with his laptop and banged on his keyboard for a majority of the day as if it owed him money. Nice work if you can get it. But I didn't dare serve him coffee or plop myself down on the seat in front of him the way my hormones demanded.

In truth, I was terrified he might see right through Bowie and spot Stella hiding there. Retired or not, he's a detective. He's got his radar sharpened to pick up even the most miniscule misgiving, and Lord knows there's nothing minuscule about my misgivings. If I'm smart, I'll find a mechanic asap and get Wanda whipped back into shape before they tow her away and I never see her again.

Once Shep packed up and went home, I asked Mud, the handyman, if he could help me find someone to look at my car and he mentioned he had a cousin who might be able to kick-start it back to life. He said he'd let me know when he got in touch with him.

No sooner does seven o'clock arrive than Opal strides in dressed to the oddball nines with a black glittery feathered number that enrobes her like a fur coat and a thick encrusted cuff of a necklace with purple and red stones.

"Come." She claps her hands and Tilly, Thea, Flo, and I gather around. "It's tea time, girls."

"We're on it!" Tilly announces as she and the girls head to the back and each emerges with a set of fine china set on large silver platters. Tilly's tea set is off-white with a spray of colorful flowers printed on the pot and teacups. Thea's china is a green damask pattern with a holiday feel, and Flo has blue and white china with tiny delicate flowers printed all over it. "Get one off the rack," Tilly barks my way. "Stitch Witchery starts in half an hour, but the women come early."

"And stay late," Opal adds as she exits the café.

I pick up an off-white set of china decorated with gold trim and dainty pink roses as I follow Tilly's lead and a small army of cute fluffy cats all the way to the library.

The library is a monolithic room with lots of dark wood shelves brimming with books, hardbacks, paperbacks, and leather-bound copies of God knows what. You name it and it's most likely in here. There's a marble reception counter to the right that looks as if it could have been used as a checkout desk once upon a time, but at the moment it's where we're laying out the tea.

In the middle of the room, several dark mahogany tables have conjoined, and there are already a few women knitting and doing other crafty-inspired things that require yarn and copious amounts of gossip.

Opal nods my way. "I insist on having the teapots refilled and reheated periodically throughout the night. Tilly has them labeled." She points as Tilly lays out a sign in front of each one—*chamomile, Earl Grey, Darjeeling, orange spice*, and *peppermint*—and the final makeshift sign reads *choose your own adventure*. Next to it sits a variety of triangular fancy teabags in a silver bowl.

"Of course, I add a little spice to mine." Opal gives a little wink as she pulls a small bottle of whiskey from the inside of her coat.

Tilly, Thea, and Flo busy themselves with the crowd at hand, asking each woman what kinds of tea they would like while I watch Opal spike her Darjeeling.

"So this is what you do?" I glance to the women pouring in. "You knit?"

"Oh, I don't knit. I tried and tangled my fingers in a knot. Tilly had to call 911. It wasn't pretty. Heavens no. I cross-stitch. It's much easier since Flo bought me a magnifying glass to use along with it."

The room begins to flood with bodies, and soon almost all the seats at the ginormous table are filled.

"Opal, you have a lot of women coming to this event. Do you charge them for it?"

"Why would I charge?" She takes a careful sip of one hundred proof Darjeeling. "It's strictly medicinal. Most of these poor things are still married to *men*." She says *men* as if it were a four-letter word and, believe me, after that Johnny debacle, I can commiserate. "I wanted to do something for the community—especially the community of women. I wanted to give them a place to come where they could complain about their miserable lives and find a comradery in one another and maybe pet a cat or two."

I think on this a moment. "And that's good. Very altruistic of you. I like that. But the businesswoman in me says we should be charging them."

"What? Oh heavens, I can't." Her dark crimson lips contort into all sorts of odd shapes. "I mean, I haven't, and if I start doing so now, they'll just find somewhere else to get together and Stitch Witchery will be no more, and horror upon horrors they may not invite me."

"You're right. You've set a precedent and it's too late to charge them admission." I glance down to that brown bottle still in her hands. "But it's not too late to switch up the menu."

She snaps her fingers. "I knew I should have brought scones and teacakes into this, but, to be truthful, the expense has held me back." She wrinkles her nose. "And no offense to the chefs at the café, but teacakes are not really their thing."

The room begins to buzz with murmurs and sporadic bouts of laughter as the women all tend to their chosen projects at hand.

"I have an idea and it doesn't involve teacakes. Trust me on this one."

"Thank you for coming tonight," I say, stepping over to the table, and the room quiets down as all eyes turn my way. "Opal wanted to extend her appreciation to all of you here and let you know that in addition to the tea and free access to the myriad of books in the library, not to mention friendly felines"—I glance her way and she nods—"you can also add a touch of comfort to your tea—for medicinal purposes, of course." I look back to Opal and she brandishes that small bottle of whiskey to the women in the room and is met with a hum of approval. "If you're interested in adding a touch of comfort to your beverage, I'll be coming around and adding just a nip. For a small fee, of course."

A sharp murmur erupts around the table as the women all talk amongst themselves. I guess it is mostly women over sixty-five, but there's a smattering of every age and they all look equally excited.

"And"—I raise my voice just a notch as all eyes revert my way—"if you've had more than a nip, Tilly, Mud, and I will gladly offer rides home. We do encourage you to select a designated driver for next week's meeting."

A blue-haired granny raises her hand. "I have a touch of a sore throat. I could use a little comfort in my tea." She quickly brandishes a couple of bills, and Opal is off to the races.

A younger woman with glasses and her hair in a bun lifts a hand as well. "I have a cough coming on and it's hard enough to teach the third grade when you're in perfect health. I'd better have a nip of comfort myself."

Soon enough, the entire room has an ailment they're ready and willing to flaunt, and Opal is forced to break into the stash she has below the reception area. Within the first twenty minutes, we're swimming in dollar bills.

"Stop salivating." Opal smacks me on the nose with the wad of bills in her hands. "It's still just fifteen percent."

"How about a bounty of a hundred off the top each time I come up with a new moneymaking venture?"

Opal tips her head and glances to the ceiling. "Okay."

"Okay? Just like that?" Obviously, I shouldn't look this glittering gift horse in the socialite mouth, but Opal hasn't been so easily accommodating. Come to think of it, it's probably the liquor that's talking.

"Okay, under one condition." She solidifies the look of a woman who has some serious business acumen. "The ideas need to be spectacular, and if they bomb on the third try, I get my money back."

I make a face. "Deal. My ideas don't bomb." That is, unless the feds or the mob gets involved. Then we'll both be on the run.

Opal takes a seat at the table and her furry Bengal cat King hops in her arms. I take a seat between Flo and Thea in hopes to go unnoticed for the next craft-riddled hour.

Flo is working on a cross-stitch project herself, a cat snuggled at the foot of a grandfather clock, and the words *time to*—followed by a salty four-letter word that I'm sure doesn't lose its charm with Flo. She grunts over to me while blowing a dark lock of hair out of her eye, her lipstick per usual matches her sooty tresses.

"Don't judge." She glowers at me. "It's going to be a pillow. I'll get to turn it over when I want to—"

"I get it," I say as I look to Thea who is happily hooking together a fuzzy rug that seems to be taking shape as a picture of a brook with a deer standing near it.

"Latch hook." She nods my way. "This is the easiest, if you ask me."

Flo grunts again, "Nope. This is the easiest. All you have to do is follow the pattern already printed on the canvas and make tiny X's in each box with the right color floss. I've got software that lets me design them any way I want."

A thought comes to me. "You mean I can have it say whatever I want?"

"Yup. You wanna make a pillow, too?"

It seems small enough. No bigger than a foot in either direction.

"Yes. Yes, I do. Same design, but how about we just have it say one word? Meow."

She shrugs. "Suit yourself. I'll have it ready by next week."

"Perfect." A twinge of excitement builds in my stomach. There has to be a way to communicate with my Uncle Vinnie. I'm sure he's worried sick. And all he needs is to hear or see the code word, *meow*. Who's to say a pillow couldn't do just that?

"Smile!" Tilly waves us to attention before snapping a picture. "Hashtag Stitch Witchery as usual." I hop out of my seat and head on over to her.

"Where are you uploading that?" My stomach spears with heat.

"Just the usual suspects. My social media sites. Don't worry." She leans in, her fingers still working their fastest to blast that evidence of my existence onto the internet. "You look amazing. I'd kill for your hair and skin." Her finger taps the screen before she holds her phone my way.

And there I am, in a crowd—but nonetheless, my face is in the wild. My God, if Johnny hasn't been apprehended by the feds yet, or killed, he could hunt me down and turn me in. I'll have to do something to remedy that pronto. And something tells me deleting that picture is the answer.

"So who's your next suspect?" She forces a smile to come and go. Tilly might be as sarcastic as they come, but for someone like me who hails from the sarcasm capital of the world, she cures my homesick blues. If I had to guess where Tilly was born and raised, I would hands down say Hastings, New Jersey. But it's nice to know they grow 'em tough as nails right here in Vermont, too.

I lean in close to her ear. "Devin thinks the manager, Richard Broadman, might have had a beef with Perry or vice versa. She thinks he was ripping Perry off."

"Ooh, Richard." Her shoulders hike up and down. "You know, I thought he would have called me by now." She makes a face.

"Don't take it personally. He's been dealing with the death of a client. And maybe covering up a murder and a wife. Hey, can I see your phone?"

She hands it over without asking a single question and I quickly look him up.

The screen populates.

"Broadman Managerial Services," I say, clicking into it.

Tilly peers over my shoulder. "Looks like his office is in Woodley—at the Cross Roads Center. I know exactly where that is. It's where I got my phone. Hey? I've got a pair of thigh-high boots I've been thinking of taking out for a spin. I'm riding shotgun."

"Tilly, it's spring. It's almost eighty degrees out today. Those thigh-high boots will melt onto your flesh."

"Oh, hon." She bites down on a devious smile. "I'm not planning on leaving them on for long." She gives a dark laugh before she stops cold as she looks to the door. "Stud muffin alert. Here comes Sexy Wexy. Why do I get the feeling he's here to see you?" She takes back her phone. "I'll be indulging a little comfort to myself if you need me."

Sure enough, Shepherd makes his way over. There's a gleam in those crystal eyes, and just the sight of him makes my insides explode with heat. His hair is dewy as if he just got out of the shower, and my fingers twitch to touch that scruff on his face. He's donned a dark dress shirt and a gray tie coupled with a pair of corduroys.

"Bowie, just the person I was hoping to see," he says as Opal comes over to join us.

"No offense, Shepherd"—she gives his tie a quick tug—"but unless you plan on knitting up a blanket, you won't be able to stay." She snaps her fingers my way and her mouth rounds out as if an idea was formulating in her mind.

"Unless, of course, you're willing to pay twenty dollars." She shrugs my way.

"Fifty," I counter.

Shep takes a breath and his chest expands to unreasonable widths.

"As good a deal as that might be, I'm afraid I won't be long." He looks my way. "I was giving a guest lecture out in Maple Grove and realized I don't have your number."

"Oh, isn't that sweet?" Opal purrs at the thought. "He wants to ask you on a proper date." She fans herself with her fingers. "Let's just say I called it."

Shep purses his lips, his glowing eyes still settled over mine. "So I could call and let you know the front door to your cabin was left ajar and a skunk found its way in and sprayed it."

"What?" I moan. "There goes my new spring wardrobe."

Shep winces. "Don't worry. I chased it away and I'm airing it out. I should probably have your number, though. You know, in the event of a skunk sighting."

"I"—your average person has a phone, and if he hasn't figure out that I'm not average yet, I'm about to give him the memo—"don't have a phone anymore. I fell into a bit of tough times and, well, it was the first casualty. My car was the second."

Shep's features soften. "You should have a phone."

"I know that," I say. "But—I don't have a credit card. I had an ex junk up my credit and now no one will touch me with a ten-foot pole. I guess I could get a burner."

Opal groans, "Everyone knows those are for thugs, dear. I'll put you on my business plan and pull it out of your paycheck."

"Oh, thank you," I say as she heads back to the tea station with a wave. "I guess I'll get Tilly to take me out to Woodley." I shrug to Shep. "That's where she said she got her phone. And she might just be a little anxious to show off a pair of thigh-high boots to one of her senior suitors."

Shep's lids hood low and an audible series of gasps emit from somewhere behind me in direct correlation to his bedroom eyes.

"Tilly's senior suitor wouldn't happen to be a man by the name of Richard Broadman, would it?"

I bite down on a smile. "Someone's done their homework. I'm starting to think you're inching your way out of retirement. Is this going to affect your pension plan?"

His lips curl on one side. "I'll be by the café at noon to pick you up."

Tilly zips by. "Sounds like a date."

I shake my head at him. "Don't worry, Shep. I know better."

"Good," he grunts as he heads out the door.

But does Shep know better?

Something tells me he's too ornery to care.

10

Shep showed up at noon like he promised and whisked me off to Woodley in his truck. He's dressed to kill in a sports coat, dress shirt, and tie, paired with chinos. Come to think of it, I haven't seen a single fashion misstep this man has made since I've been here. But, then again, with a face like that, not too many people notice his clothes.

Woodley County is lined with oaks and maples and still manages to have a small-town appeal despite the big city hub of office buildings and shopping plazas squatting over every city block.

Shep leads us into Woodley Mobile and I pick out a smart phone that can do everything but fly. And just as I'm about to check out, the service member helping me informs me that I can't just add myself onto Opal's plan.

"Well, there's that," I say to Shep. "I guess I'll have to come back with Opal."

"That won't be necessary." Shep expels a sigh that either signals his pity for me or his genuine irritation. I'm betting on the latter. "I can put you on my plan. It's not a big deal."

"Really? Thank you. I'm good for the money." That's most likely not true, but it felt like the right thing to say. And putting me on his phone plan? That's more of a commitment than I ever got from any of my exes.

"And I know where to find you to get it." He flashes a short-lived smile, and before you know it, I'm back in the technological swing of things with the rest of humanity now that I have the sum total of human history right at my fingertips.

We take off, and as soon as we hit the fresh air, I step in front of him to block his path.

"Thank you, Shep. You didn't have to do that. I guess you have a beating heart after all."

"Don't go spreading rumors. Besides, Opal doesn't drive. I was probably going to have to give her a ride. You saved me a trip."

"In that case, I'll not only pay what I owe for the phone, I'll throw in a little extra for gas."

"It's on me. Ready to head back?"

I glance a few doors down, and there it is, Broadman Managerial Services.

"No," he says it flat without missing a beat because clearly my ogling eyes have made my nefarious intentions obvious.

"Yes," I counter. "We're right here. I can stop in and tell him I'm inquiring about his services for a friend. And while I'm there, I'll ask a few questions about his relationship with Perry."

His brows hike and he looks momentarily amused, handsome as a heart attack in the process, too, but that's another matter entirely.

"That's not how an investigation works, Bowie. If he's guilty, he'll suspect something. If he's innocent, he might think he's being accused of something and leave town. Either way, it could grind the real investigation to a halt."

"The real investigation that your ex, Detective Grimsley, is conducting—or the unofficial investigation you're conducting?"

"I'm not conducting an investigation. I'm simply curious to see if I can help move things along."

"Great news, Shep. You can. Follow my lead." I'm about to stomp in the direction of the management company when a tall, handsome, older man with a shock of white hair jogs out of the building and heads a few doors down to a donut shop.

I smack Shep on the stomach and bark out a laugh.

"Looks like we caught him in the middle of a carb attack. Come on." I motion for him to follow and he gently reels me back by the wrist. "I suddenly have a hankering for a hot apple fritter."

"We can't just walk in there. Who eats donuts at one in the afternoon?"

"We do." I all but drag Shep along as we enter the Donut Dungeon.

Not sure what the owner was trying to achieve with a name like that, but I'm not here to debate the virtues of an inviting moniker. I'm here to nab a killer.

We spot Richard up front picking out his sweet treats while a young girl behind the counter tries to keep up with his demands and shoves them into a box.

Back in Hastings, I helped run the donut shop and a car wash for one of Johnny's uncles. That's where the illegal green river flowed and where I tried to sop up a little of that green goop for myself. And here I am on the run in another donut shop entirely. Why does it feel as if it's all come full circle?

"Follow my lead," I whisper to Shep just as a fresh-faced teenage boy comes up and offers to take our order. "My boyfriend and I just had a big fight," I say a touch too loud and garner Richard's attention just the way I hoped to. "He wanted to buy me a bouquet of roses to make up for it, but I told him the only way to my heart was through a bouquet of donuts."

Both employees share a laugh before shooting down any hopes of getting a donut bouquet so I settle for a box. Shep and I decided to do a dozen mixed and let the employee pick them out.

"Fun fact"—I say to Shep, but I'm still speaking loud enough for Richard to hear without feeling as if he were eavesdropping—"I dated a guy once who gifted me a pickle bouquet after our first fight."

Shep's brows pinch together. "Did you take him back or sue?"

"Ha-ha," I bleat without the proper enthusiasm. "Hey?" I take a few steps toward Richard. "Don't I know you?"

He lifts his chin and looks at me from his silver-framed glasses.

"You look vaguely familiar, but I can't seem to place it." He leans in as if hoping I'd pop into focus.

"The Starry Falls Manor." I snap my fingers his way. "Opal Mortimer's place."

Shep leans in. "It's the Mortimer Manor," he whispers hot in my ear. "Sign fell off last winter."

The urge to shiver hits hard and I bite down on my lower lip as I resist it. Why is it that anything that man whispers, my body insists on translating into a sweet nothing?

I nod over to Richard. "There was a murder at the Mortimer Manor the other"—I suck in a breath. "That's right. You were the manager. I think we met. I work at the Manor Café."

"I'm sorry, I hardly remember you." Richard takes a full breath as he looks from Shep to me. "I've been a wreck ever since. I hope business at the manor wasn't hurt. I've known Opal for a few years. That was nice of her to let us use it as a venue."

"Business has been brisk," I tell him. "Poor Perry, though. I heard through the rumor mill he wasn't getting along with a few people. Do you know if they caught the killer?"

Richard's cheeks turn a flush shade of pink. "Can't say that the sheriff's department found anyone as of yet. The detective said she'd give me a call if there was a break in the case." He holds out his hand. "Let's do this again, and I'll do my best to remember it this time. Richard Broadman."

"Bowie Binx." I shake his hand and he shakes Shep's as well.

"Shepherd Wexler."

Richard makes an odd honking sound, but judging by the sudden look of glee on his face, I'd guess it was a good thing.

"*The* Shepherd Wexler?" Richard marvels. "As in S.J. Wexler who pens the Manon Tate novels?"

"One and the same." Shep sheds a short-lived smile. I've learned in the short time I've known him that those smiles are hard-won and far between.

Two pink boxes are shoved our way at the very same time and Richard and Shep both ante up at the register.

Richard nods to a booth by the window as he looks to Shep. "If you don't mind, how about five minutes where I can pick your brain? I'm a big fan of your novels. I'll admit, I'm a bit starstruck at the moment."

Starstruck? I'm starting to think Shep is a bigger deal than I understand. And personally, I'm glad I don't understand it. It's bad enough he's got that rugged exterior, those intimidating good looks. If I added another dimension to his mystique, I might just be too intimidated to talk to him.

Oh heck, who am I kidding?

I've never been intimidated by a man in all my life.

I glance to Shep and my stomach squeezes tight, letting me know he just might be the exception to the rule.

We take a seat at the booth and Richard wastes no time trying to pull a few upcoming plotlines from the author at hand.

I nosh on a glazed cruller while listening in on their conversation and contemplate the madness I'm hearing.

"Wait a minute," I say. "You're telling me that Manon, this main character of yours, is an undercover cop working within the mob? *And* he's a made man? *Pfft*." I avert my gaze. "That's not reality."

Richard grunts as if I had mortally wounded him. "But it's a work of fiction."

"You got that right," I snip.

"Wait a minute." Shep leans back in his seat. "What do you mean, it wouldn't happen? I do extensive research for my novels."

"Well, I'm here to tell you, your research is wrong." I take another bite of my cruller before freeing the apple fritter from the pink prison it's in.

"It can't be wrong." Shep lowers his lids a notch, those icy eyes pinned right over mine, and I can feel the oven-hot heat radiating from him as he sits dangerously close. "I worked with several ex-mobsters to get the details right."

I blink over at him. "And they let you get away with that whole wearing a wire to *every* family meeting bit? I'm telling you, the guy would have been fitted with cement boots after chapter three. I have a feeling the ex-mobsters you spoke with were having a little fun with you. They might squeak to save their necks, but they're pretty die-hard as far as protecting the organization as a whole. It's an unwritten code." I shove the fritter into my face and try to savor every doughy bite.

Richard nods to Shep with a show of enthusiasm in his eyes. "So who'd you get to speak with? I'm a big mafioso buff myself. Anyone newsworthy?"

Shep's shoulders bounce. "A couple of small-time thugs in for racketeering."

"Aren't they all in for that?" I say it mostly to myself as I shake my head. My father was small-time, but he's locked up nonetheless.

Shep looks to Richard. "Leftie Louis, a guy by the name of Magnificent, and a man that's known as The Sunday Sinner."

I swallow the cruller down the wrong pipe and cough up a storm as I buck and writhe just hearing Shep say my father's somewhat sinful moniker.

An employee brings me a cup of water and I quickly down it all, hoping against hope that when I pull the paper cup away from my face I would have somehow landed back in Hastings, and everything wrong with my life would have been nothing more than a bad dream. But that doesn't happen. Instead, I'm looking right into Shepherd Wexler's concerned eyes and a part of me is glad that New Jersey is still three whole states away.

I clear my throat as I look to Richard. "There was a rumor floating around the night of Perry's murder that you felt he owed you something." I'm paraphrasing from Devin and buffering it with a lie, of course. She didn't float that rumor until I cornered her at the Tumbleweed, but Richard doesn't have to know that.

Richard's jaw clenches. "And I can only guess who started that rumor, but I don't have to guess. That pretty little blonde has been spreading those rumors for months." He pegs Devin with it right out of the gate. "I guess it's not a rumor if it's true, though, now is it? Perry had a few side gigs he wasn't cutting me in on. Sure, I knew about it. Everyone knew. Perry and I exchanged words, but we were men about it. The show had to go on. I thought we had smoothed over that bump. I wasn't angry enough to gun the poor kid down. I've got my finances in order. I didn't need his. I was doing him a favor, not the other way around."

Shep offers a mournful smile. "How did you hear about these gigs he was getting on the side?"

"Nicki. His personal assistant, Nicki Magnolia. She does his scheduling and gave me a copy whenever I asked. At least up until six weeks ago. I think Perry asked her to keep me in the dark. I guess you could say, things were strained toward the end there."

A thick bout of silence fills the air before Shepherd invites Richard to his signing tomorrow night, and Richard lets out a whoop as if he just scored every number in the Powerball.

"Say"—he leans that shock of white hair our way—"your agent wouldn't happen to be coming to the signing as well, would he? I've been thinking about branching out into books."

"Why yes, *she* will be there."

I caught the emphasis he put on *she*. It doesn't surprise me Shep has surrounded himself with women. He's a smart man after all.

Richard takes off and we take our box and hop into Shep's truck.

"Well, Detective Binx?" He looks my way. "What do you think?"

"I think you have a fan for life. And maybe a stalker at your next book signing." That vision I had of Shep being attacked by a blonde comes to mind. "You wouldn't happen to have security with you when you do those things, do you?"

He pulls back the right side of his jacket and exposes a gun holster with the butt of a small black pistol sticking out.

"A leftover relic from your investigative days?" I don't bother adding a hint of sarcasm to my words.

"A relic that I won't be parting with anytime soon."

"Good," I say. "You never know when you might need it." Like, say, tomorrow night. "Did you get the feeling that Perry was about to let Richard go? I mean, Richard said Perry asked his personal assistant to stop feeding him his schedule. Sounds like there was a pretty big rift there. Richard and Perry weren't getting along. Hatred could certainly be a motive for murder."

Shep steadies his gaze out the windshield. "Maybe. Something tells me Nicki might be able to fill me in on the rest of the story."

"You mean fill *me* in on it. We women have a natural bond. She'll trust me more. Besides, I've already befriended her."

He looks my way and scowls. "I'll befriend her."

"I bet you will."

We drive back to Starry Falls in silence, and all the while I think about my father meeting Shepherd Wexler long before I did.

What a small, small world, and I don't mean that in any good way.

11

Thursday night, the Book Basement is bustling with bodies.

The shop itself is adorably cozy with dark bookshelves lining the walls, tables of books strewn around the front, and an entire table dedicated to S.J. Wexler's bestsellers. Apparently, there are a lot of them. There's a huge framed poster with a black and white picture of his scowling, yet arrestingly good-looking face, and next to that is an entire litany of bestseller lists he's dominated. Nice to know the resident snoop, aka my new landlord, is such an accomplished author. I crane my neck toward the back where he's currently speaking with the store manager, and the entire room seems to be hyperaware of his presence.

Rows of folding chairs are set out, each with a body already warming it. There's a podium near the back where Shep just stepped up to, ready to read from his latest, greatest work. The bookstore itself is dimly lit, and judging by the litany of electric candles set out everywhere you look, it seems to be a purposeful endeavor. A refreshment table to the right boasts of free coffee, and the scent of fresh hot java combined with sweet paperbacks is a heady combination.

Opal and Tilly pop up next to me, each with a copy of his new book in hand, *A Made Man*, and I can't help but avert my eyes.

"Where's your book?" Opal sounds a bit panicked for me. Her silver locks look as if they've been freshly blown out for the occasion. She's donned a black beaded gown that touches the floor. And for reasons only Opal can explain, she's chosen to pair it with a leather choker with tiny metal studs. But, now that I know that particular biker-inspired accessory is in her possession, I might just ask to borrow it for myself.

"I didn't buy a book," I whisper. "No offense, but I don't exactly have a spare twenty-four ninety-nine lying around at the moment."

Tilly gives a husky laugh. "Oh, hon, I think he's going to gift you an entire stack of his bestsellers." She nods. "As soon as you gift him a little something." Her shoulders wiggle, making her chest jiggle, and I get the naughty implications.

I glance back in his direction. "I'm not gifting him a pound of flesh. Besides, I don't even think he'd be interested in receiving it. He's not exactly throwing out any green lights."

Tilly waves me off. "Shep Wexler has been living in the red-light district for so long, I doubt he realizes some women still look for a signal every now and again. Word on the street has it, if you want a piece of Shep, you just throw yourself at him." Her shoulders jerk. "That's what I did."

"What? *Eww*." I swat her on the arm and she breaks out into a cackle. "I did not want to know that."

Opal bounces her tresses in her palm. "Then I won't tell you what the two of us did."

I gasp as I lean toward Tilly. "She's kidding, right?"

The lights go on and off and a murmur of excitement stirs the room to life as last-minute stragglers search for a seat to call their own. The rest of the people here are forced to stand on the sidelines and, in truth, I'm voluntarily doing so in the event I need to make a quick exit. There is only so much mobster folklore I can handle. I'm a little over the hard facts, too.

"Do you ladies remember what we talked about?" I hitch my head at Opal and Tilly. Earlier today, I reminded them of that vision I had of Shep being strangled by some obsessed blonde. It's not like I could have called the police and warned them that some nutcase was about to descend on the book signing.

Opal gives a solemn nod. "I'll flank him on the right."

Tilly bats her lashes. "On his right or your right? Because if it's his right, then it's your left—and I'm doing left, remember?"

"It doesn't matter. Just go in different directions," I say in an effort to keep it neat. I suck in a quick breath. "I almost forgot to tell you, I had another vision."

Opal leans in. "About Shep again? Oh my God, was he dead? I've seen enough dead bodies for a lifetime." She starts to fan herself with the hardback in her hand and nearly knocks herself out.

"Careful," I say, pulling her hand down a notch. "And no, it was about Devin O'Malley, Perry Flint's blonde bombshell of a girlfriend. I saw her with clothes disheveled and she looked right at me and said, 'Okay, fine. You caught me. I'm guilty. Are you happy? Perry left me no choice. I had to do it. He forced my hand. And you're not going to tell anyone, you hear me?'"

Tilly's mouth falls opens. "She did it! All we need to do is trap her into confessing."

Opal prods me with her book. "Where do you think the two of you were when she said that? Maybe we can hasten it into happening?"

"I don't know. All I was aware of was her and that disheveled look she was sporting. But regardless, even if she does confess to me, it doesn't mean she won't change her tune when it comes to the sheriff's department. We need evidence if we want to bump her up to the top of the suspect list." I wrinkle my nose at Opal. "By the way, you and I are on it."

"Oh?" Her heavily drawn-in eyes light up. "Did I get top billing?"

I make a face. "No, but you should have."

"Thank you." She taps me on the arm. "I knew I liked you."

The crowd grows quiet as we quickly scuttle to our places and I bump into a body.

"Oh, sorry," I say, backing up, only to find myself face to face with an all too familiar detective. "*Nora*."

She smacks her lips. "I prefer Detective Grimsley." Her dark hair is pulled back into its signature bun and she's wearing a pink frosty lipstick that washes her out, but I'll be the last person to mention it because a woman should feel free to wear whatever color lipstick she likes when she's packing heat and handcuffs.

"I'm so glad you're here," I pant with relief. "I mean, you know, in the event some lunatic tries to attack Shep. You're sort of the first line of defense. You'd think they'd have security at these kinds of events, but it seems no one really cares about his safety except for you."

"I don't care all that much either." She gives a sly wink.

"Funny. But I get it. I have an ex that I would pay to see some crazed maniac attack. But, thankfully, you've taken an oath to serve and protect. And judging by all the hyperventilating women here tonight, I suggest you remain on high alert." And that way I won't be forced to use the zip ties I stuffed in my new-to-me Louis Vuitton bag. I was a little apprehensive to use them to begin with.

I've spent most of my life as a virtual magnet for trouble. The last thing I need to be doing is arresting members of the general public with plastic handcuffs that need to be cut off with scissors.

Besides, I'm already at the top of the list in a murder investigation. And believe me, I would have gladly given Opal that honor. In fact, she can have top billing in just about everything. I'm supposed to be laying low and avoiding the radar for Pete's sake, not starring in a crime drama and carrying around plastic restraints in the event a bombshell attacks the cute boy in class.

Nora attempts to step around me, but I block her path.

"Where are you going?" I hiss without meaning to.

Her forehead furrows with enough worry lines to let me know I'm the one who should be worried.

"Up front. I like to see him sweat. Now, if you'll excuse me."

"Okay, but remember, stay vigilant."

She makes a face as she blows right past me.

Shepherd taps the mic and the room explodes into titters as if that's all they needed to alleviate the pent-up frustration they've been harboring all night. If I'm not mistaken, I think I just heard about a dozen ovaries pop in his honor.

Shep welcomes the crowd and slides in a little self-abasing humor just as a stunning brunette walks in and begins to sashay her way down the aisle as if this were her wedding day. Regina Valentine looks as if she just strutted out of the pages of a glossy magazine with her chestnut hair, long and flowing, and a tight white dress that's cut down to there in the front and sitting up to here in the back. And honest to God, the only thing I can think about is when is she donating that sucker? I bet she trashes her wardrobe seasonally. If I'm lucky, New Year's Eve will see me in white.

I blink back at my own odd thought. I'm not planning on being here through the new year. I'm not even supposed to be here through the *weekend*. The plan was to fix Wanda and hightail it to our neighbors in the Great White North.

Shep says something that has the room tittering once again, and I give a quivering smile as if I heard it.

Those hypnotic pale blue eyes of his latch onto mine, and for a moment I feel as if I'm the only woman in the room. He leans into the mic, his gaze never leaving mine, and he says something I miss because I'm too busy swooning. The room lights up with laughter twice as riotous as before. Figures. I was probably the butt of some dumb joke. And I'm starting to feel like just that.

He tilts his head my way. "In all seriousness, the themes explored in my latest book, *A Made Man*, are those of redemption, a new beginning, taking chances on something you never thought you'd have, and embracing change when it's right in front of you." The birth of a sly smile crests his lips as he nods my way.

Am I the change?

My cheeks heat so much they can rival the surface of the sun.

Shep goes on to read chapter one and I can't help but note he has the rapt attention of every woman in this room and the few men that bothered to show. The chapter seems to be dragging a bit, so I leave my post and head for the coffee station. I've always been a sucker for a free cup of just about anything, and so much more now that I have just about nothing.

I glance back at Shep as I take a careful sip of what tastes like the world's best cup of coffee, so creamy and smooth. I'll have to make a point to give a cup to Opal. We really need to up our java game at the café if we want to corner the coveted soccer mom demographic. I've got some solid ideas to help build both her revenue and mine. And it's high time I implement them. With her financial backing, of course. I'm guessing an espresso machine doesn't come cheap.

Shep thanks the audience for coming out, and the manager of the place steals the mic to let them know Shep will be mingling with the audience before we get to the signing portion of the evening.

Soon, Shep is engulfed with a crowd of women, and their shared laughter echoes off the walls.

And that's when I see her.

A quick moving blonde zips in through the doors, weaving her way through the sea of limbs as she darts right for him.

"It's her!" I shout to no one in particular as I traverse people and folding chairs alike in an effort to save Shep's life.

The blonde wraps her hands around his neck and begins to throttle him just the way it played out in my mind's eye and I catch a glimpse of Opal running in the opposite direction in a panic, while Tilly is riding her leg up one of the male employee's sides as if she were looking to score a little more than a couple free bookmarks.

Geez.

If you want something done, you have to do it yourself.

"Aargggh!" I run, shrieking, as I grab a fistful of her hair and try my hardest to pluck her off him, but since that tried-and-true tactic I've used since the seventh grade doesn't seem to be working, I do the only other thing I can think of. I dump my coffee over the two of them.

The woman shrieks right back and lets an entire litany of salty words—and a few blatant threats—fly. But I don't bother with a comeback. Instead, I whip those zip ties out of my purse and hog-tie her with her arms behind her back and her ankles to her wrists.

Okay, confession: I may have fantasized about doing just this to Johnny right before I threw him over the tallest bridge in Jersey to a watery death below. It's still my favorite go-to mental escape when I need to relax my jangled nerves.

"What the hell, Shep?" the woman yelps up at him.

I land my fists to my hips as I pant a smile his way.

"You're welcome," I say as his eyes round out in horror.

A hard tap comes over my shoulder and I turn to see Tilly shaking her head at me.

"Bowie?" She grimaces my way. "I don't know how to break this to you, but that woman you just tied up like a Thanksgiving turkey is his sister."

"*What?*" I jump back in horror as Nora pops up.

"All right, Shep," she says, looking my way. "How much evidence do you need before you see I was right? The girl is a lunatic." She pulls out a Swiss army knife and cuts Shep's poor sister loose. "I told you I had a bad feeling about her. And now look what she's done."

A bad feeling?

"I'm so sorry." My fingers fly to my lips as Shep helps his sister up. Her hair sort of has this tumbleweed thing happening, and her lipstick is smeared clear across her cheek, and as much as I'd like to believe this weathered look she's sporting isn't entirely my fault, I'm afraid it is.

Shep lands a stern expression my way. "Kelly, this is Bowie Binx. She's new in town."

The woman bats her lashes my way forcefully and slowly, cluing me in on the fact she's not all that happy with me.

"Kelly, did you say?" I tug at a lock of my hair until it hurts. "So nice to meet you. Sorry if that was a little rough. I'm from Connecticut. That's how we greet one another."

Was there really anything else to say?

Those icy blue eyes she has in common with Shep burn a hole right through me.

"*I'm* from Connecticut," she seethes. "And that is most certainly *not* how we greet each other."

Crap.

Shep pulls his lips back in what I'm hoping is a smile—although I've yet to see one from him, so it's not as if I can be conclusive about that.

"I'm sure Bowie has a good explanation." He rocks back on his heels as if he were ready to hear it.

The manager comes by and quickly shuttles him over to the signing table. And his sister waves a special finger at me as she takes off, too.

I spend the rest of the night watching as miles of women sigh and swoon in Shep's presence.

Soon enough, the tired, huddled masses of estrogen stream back out onto Main Street while Shep enjoys a lively conversation with his sister and Nora.

Tilly gives Opal and me a ride home, dropping me off first, and I sit out on the bench in front of my cabin, watching the stars in the sky as they glitter like broken glass. For some reason, Hastings seemed devoid of any constellations, and now I know why. Starry Falls has been hogging them all to herself this whole while. She all but confesses the starry heist right there in her moniker.

The sound of footsteps shuffling in this direction startles me back to life as Shep makes his way over with a copy of his book in hand.

"Thought maybe you might have wanted one of these." He passes it to me, and I stand as I take it. "It's signed by the author. I hear he's a little full of himself, so I don't blame you for not waiting in that line tonight."

My lips invert as I try to hide a smile. "Is that what you wanted?" I whisper as I take a step close to him. "Me, standing in a line fifty deep, while I wait my turn at bat?"

His cheek hikes up on one side. "You do realize how that sounded."

"I was simply pointing out a fact. Your dirty mind took it elsewhere."

He gives a long blink and nods. "Before I forget, I suggest you leave the zip ties at home next time. Restraining people against their will could land *you* in restraints."

"Fine. But for the record, I thought she was attacking you."

He takes a breath as he examines me, and I can feel my skin pricking under the heat of his stare.

"You were protecting me. I like that." He gives a little wink before heading off. "Goodnight, Bowie. "

"Thanks for the book!"

I open it to the first page to get a look at his signature, and there's an inscription up top. *To Bowie, I have never met a soul like you. Stay different.* Underneath that there's a squiggle of a signature.

"Stay different?" I mutter. "Hey?" I call out. "Is this an insult?"

"Goodnight," he says as he closes the door behind him.

He's never met a soul like me.

Darn tootin'.

I don't need Shepherd Wexler's affection. I don't need the affection of anyone in this town. In fact, once I clear both my name and Opal's, I'm going to demand Wanda come out of her automotive coma and take me to Canada, or I'll borrow one of Opal's brooms and fly there.

Come tomorrow, I'm going to track down Nicki Magnolia, and she's going to tell me everything she knows about that grievance between Perry and Richard—and anything she knows about Devin, too. That vision I had is bound to come true. It's as good as a confession.

I glance to the cabin Shep just stalked off to.

If only he knew how different I was.

Nora was right to have a bad feeling about me.

Heck, right about now, I do, too.

12

"Two words," I say as I look Opal Mortimer in the eye. "Naked Pilates."

She squints into me with those raccoon eyes of hers and her lipstick a touch too orange as we stand in the café after the lunch rush pushed through.

Her brows hike. "Exactly who is going to be naked in this scenario?"

"*You.* You're going to teach it," I'm quick to inform her. "And, of course, the students will be naked, too. You won't be alone. But where you'll draw the big bucks is in the secret viewing area we're going to install in the next room."

Mud belts out a goofy laugh. "Where do I sign up for this delight?" His blond hair has that electrocution thing going on, and judging by the way he's been giggling like a teenage girl all morning, his brain is fried, too.

Opal plucks off her little white gloves and smacks me on the arm with them.

"No can do. I never did have a thing for pilots, clothed or otherwise. Back to the think tank with you."

Shep catches my eye as he sips his fourth cup of coffee while contemplating his next literary move, or mistake for that matter. I cherry-picked my way through that book he gave me and he's painted the entire mob to be a caricature of its cartoon self.

I pick up a fresh carafe and head on over, but I'm not interested in filling his cup to the brim more than I am picking his brain. I take a seat across from him and Opal plops down next to me.

Opal sags over her coffee. "I miss money." She elongates each word in that socialite twang of hers I'm beginning to envy.

Shep glances up at the two of us and his lips curl at the tips.

"What's happening here?"

I lean in. "I just wanted to apologize again for momentarily restraining your sister. Is she really from Connecticut?"

"She was." He dips his chin a notch and lands those comely peepers over me.

As much as I hate myself for it, there is an undeniable animal attraction that Shepherd Wexler exudes. Every woman knows it. I can't fault myself for falling under his animalistic spell.

He pulls his coffee close. "She moved back to Maple Grove last year."

"Nice," I say. "And it was nice to see she was so supportive of your work last night. Along with every woman in Starry Falls." I meant for it to come out cute and funny, and instead, it came out passive-aggressive and rife with jealousy. "Sorry, that sort of didn't come out exactly the way I envisioned."

Opal waves me off as she pulls her mug to her lips. "Just about every woman in that room was his ex." She gives a sly wink over to him. "Isn't that right, Shepherd? How did it feel having all of your discarded paramours lining up to see you? I can only imagine that's quite a mind bender." She sighs. "And back to me now." She groans my way. "When are these surefire ways of putting me back in the financial swing of things going to take effect?"

Shep blinks over at me. "You're going to put her back in the financial swing of things?"

My mouth falls open. "What's that supposed to mean? You don't think I'm capable?" An incredulous laugh huffs from me. "You don't know half the things I'm capable of."

Shep frowns as he toasts me with his mug. "That's exactly what I'm afraid of."

Tilly traipses over. "Did I miss anything?"

"No," I'm quick to inform her. "I was just about to ask our resident private dick here if he knew where I could find Nicki Magnolia."

Shep's brows slowly rise as if he were amused or percolating with anger. With him you never can tell.

He clears his throat. "And why would you want to find Ms. Magnolia?"

Tilly scoffs. "So she can quiz her." She jabs his arm with her elbow. "It's no wonder you quit the homicide division. You were awful at it. Anyone can see Bowie is determined to catch that killer."

Shep gives a long blink. "I didn't quit. I retired." He looks my way. "And I'm fully aware of why you want to speak with Nicki. I get it. You're worried. You're on the suspect list and you're in a panic to find whoever did this to clear your name."

"And hers." I point to Opal.

Shep nods. "You're a good friend, Bowie. But there's no need for you to put yourself in danger. Nora and I can handle this."

"Ooh." Opal wiggles her chest and that silver blouse she's donned shimmers like a disco ball. "Sounds like someone is using this homicide as a means to get back on the love nest express with his ex."

Both Tilly and I gasp in horror.

"Gross." Tilly shoots him a look. "I'm talking about you and Nora, not that whole using the dead guy. Personally, I think dragging a dead body into a relationship could spice a few things up."

The three of us offer her a morbid stare.

"What?" She blinks our way as if trying to make sense of it. "That was weird, wasn't it? I think I see a customer up front. Buh-bye." She scuttles off, and Opal tosses a hand in the air.

"Murder," she jeers. "Why didn't I think of that? If I would have killed my ex, I wouldn't be in this financial pickle right now."

"Right," I say. "You'd be in a prison cell."

She brushes me off with a roll of the eyes. "Nonsense. I would have gotten creative. I'll have you know, I can be a crafty little vixen when I want to. I would have poisoned his coffee or locked him in the closet with a couple of rabid coyotes. Oh, the possibilities were endless, and now look at me. I've squandered a perfectly good opportunity to become a legend among women everywhere."

"Well, if you got creative, I'm pretty sure no one would know. I mean, that's the point, right? Getting away with something."

"And have it all be for nothing?" She takes a sip from her coffee. "Heavens no. I would write a tell-all and give it to my old butler, telling him not to hit publish until an hour after my death. That way those who want to praise me could still do so at my viewing. Anyway, that's all blood under the bridge as they say." She leans my way. "But you're still young. Don't be like me. You start plotting your future husband's demise right now, young lady. I'll give you that advice for free." She gives my cheek a quick pinch before heading off, and Shep shakes his head my way.

"Don't do it, Bowie. Her advice might be free, but you'll have to pay another way."

"Why? Because no good deed goes unpunished?"

Shep lets out a heavy breath as if he were exasperated with me. "Because no criminal goes unpunished."

"You really believe that? I'm almost amused."

"Yes, I believe that. Just because I've retired doesn't mean I've stopped believing in our judicial system. And I believe in something more than that. I believe people may get away with something for so long, but eventually, we all have to pay the piper."

I swallow hard at the thought.

If Shep is right, that means my days are numbered.

He nods my way. "Are you dropping this incessant need to put away Perry Flint's killer?"

"No," I reply without pausing. "Whoever did this is thumbing their nose at the sheriff's department. And that old girlfriend you're chumming up with again happens to have a vendetta against me. I can see it in her wily eyes." I make a face. "And please don't tell me you're really using this case to get back into her good graces. That is sick, by the way. Just pick up the phone and ask her to lunch, dinner, or dessert at your place with nothing more than a can of whipped cream. You're S.J. Wexler. You can have any woman you want."

"Any woman?" He tips his head my way.

"What exactly are you implying?"

"I think you're trying to change the subject."

A sharp laugh belts from me. "I think *you're* trying to change the subject." A thought comes to me and I whip out that shiny new cell phone the ornery ex-officer across from me landed in my greedy little hands. "I bet Nicki is all over social media displaying where she is, putting a time stamp on it and giving me a map to the place." Sure enough, Nicki's signature dark bun appears on my screen and I click into her account. "Ah-ha! Look at this. It says hashtag scrapbooking. Hashtag Sterling Lake Public Library." I click onto the library hashtag and it leads me to their events page. "Well, well. It looks as if they're having a scrapbooking event all day. I bet Tilly has a ton of old pictures she'd just love for me to organize."

"No, she doesn't." Shep strums his fingers before me. "You don't have any business going down there."

"You don't tell me what I can and can't do. My ex tried that with me once, and you don't want to know what happened to him." I zip across the café, and Tilly is just about to hand over the keys to her car when Shep strides up, briefcase in hand, a fresh scowl on his face.

"No need to involve Tilly." He frowns my way. "I happen to be heading that way myself."

"Whew!" Tilly mockingly wipes her brow. "I was just kidding about having a box full of Jessie's baby pictures."

"Oh." I cringe. "Is it because nobody has film anymore?"

"No"—she shakes her head—"it's because all my old pictures are of me." She gives a sassy smile. "Now, you kids go off to the library and make out or whatever it is people do in there these days. I'll make sure the customers have a good time." She unbuttons her blouse a notch.

Opal lifts a finger my way. "And if you find another body, Bowie, for God's sake, pick his pockets this time. They don't really need cold hard cash where they're going." She takes an angry bite off her croissant.

"Will do," I say as Shep and I head out into the warm Starry Falls afternoon. "What should we bring to the scrapbook event we're about to attend?"

His cheek rises on one side. "I have an idea I think you'll approve of."

But that mischievous twinkle in his eyes tells me I won't.

13

Sterling Lake is a ritzy town, where judging by all the expansive luxury mansions, you need to achieve a certain tax bracket just to drive through the place.

Lucky for me, Shep knows his way around this glitzy place and lands us right in front of the Sterling Lake Public Library. I pick up the backpack where I scooped up all of the pseudo-scrapbooking supplies, or lack thereof, that Shep was able to give me.

The inside of the library looks more like an upscale department store, with steel counters, white glossy floors and tables, and clean lines everywhere you look.

I lean toward Shep. "Is it me, or does it feel as if this place gives off a space-age feel?"

His cheek flickers. "It does have an intergalactic vibe. Here's hoping Nicki will beam up the info we need on the killer."

There are mobs of women here today from every age and stage of life as they lay out their photos before them like playing cards. Each and every one of them has a serious look on their face as they carry on hushed conversations with those around them.

"Hey, look." I nod to the table to our right. "There she is." Nestled among a handful of women sits Nicki with her hair up in a ponytail. Her pink lips are twisted to the side as she gives serious thought to her scrapbooking ways.

"Okay," I whisper. "I'm going in."

"I'm going in, too."

"No, you're not." I look at him as if he were insane. "There's not a single man at that table."

He inches back as he glances around. "There are two men over at that table." He points left. "I'll simply even out the testosterone."

"No, you won't. You'll cause a hormonal scene. It's what you do. Believe me, once the women in this room sniff you out, there won't be a quiet ovary in the house."

His lids hood dangerously low and his lips curl just a hint.

"Eat it up, buddy," I say. "But you're not sitting with us. Why don't you go off and stalk yourself or something? I bet they've got a nice selection of your mob light books."

"Did you just say mob light?" He steps back to get a better look at me.

"Yup. That's what they are. You should read 'em and weep. I have. And I bet the mob has, too."

"This is the second time you've contested the quality of my work. What makes you such an expert on the mob?"

"I"—my mouth contorts into twelve different shapes, all of them denoting a little bit of my guilt—"am a good guesser. And I'm guessing half of those things you put in there are nothing but stereotypes."

"Do you know where they get most stereotypes? From the truth."

"Not really." I close my eyes a moment because I have no problem correcting him. "They get most stereotypes from half a lie. The truth is, most mobsters are pretty decent guys who happen to love their families—I'm guessing." Hastings and everything I've left behind comes rushing to the forefront of my mind and a shudder rides through me. "Never mind. I'm off to scrapbook within an inch of my life in an effort to nail a killer. Wish me luck." I take off and Shep keeps pace with me right up until a mob of women sniff out those pheromones that are dripping off him like honey, and soon enough he has an entire fan base surrounding him, demanding he do an impromptu reading of one of his books. They cage him in at the next table over and I shoot him a look that says *told you so*.

"Is this seat taken?" I ask no one in particular as I land next to Nicki. No use in playing coy. For all I know, Nicki has a nail appointment in fifteen minutes.

"Nope. It's all yours," she says without looking my way.

"Great." I quickly dump the photos out of my bag that Shep supplied, along with the old album he dug out of his garage, and quickly pull a few pictures out. They were already snug in their own compartment, but we thought it'd look more authentic if I were actually piecing the album together with everyone else.

I glance over at the seemingly organized chaos in front of the suspect at hand and a breath hitches in my throat. An oversized album is set out in front of her with an array of fun, colorful pieces of heavy stock paper, but it's not that nor the bevy of stickers and cutouts of shapes, or the confetti, or the rainbow of pens that she has laid out that has me holding my breath. It's the fact every single one of her pictures is of Perry Flint.

She looks my way momentarily before doing a double take up at me.

"Bindi?"

"*Bowie.*" I swallow hard as I look at the poor man's smiling face strewn around the table haphazardly. "Wow, you must have really loved him." I nod to the print she's holding of Perry with the two of them at a cookout of some sort, a luau to be exact.

"Oh, this?" She blows out a heavy breath and seems to be at a loss for words. I catch her looking over at the gaggle of photos I just laid out myself and she squints over at them as if she couldn't believe her eyes either.

"It's my boyfriend." I shrug over at her, hoping she'll buy the lie. Every single picture in front of me happens to be of Shepherd Wexler's unduly handsome mug. And just for the record, he looks mean in every single one of them. "I'm making this for his mom." An easy smile starts to glide over my face before it stops cold because for the life of me I can't remember if that's the person his father is in prison for killing. Wait, it was the stepmother, right? I wince over in his direction. It's not exactly the type of thing you want to bring up again, even if it is for clarification purposes.

"Oh, right." She looks down at the hundreds of pictures of Perry floating around. "That's funny, because I'm actually doing this for his family, too. They're just sick over everything that's happened. His mother asked if I had a few pictures for the family album and I thought, *boy, do I ever*. My sister is the big scrapbooker in the family and she's the one that told me about this thing the library does, so here I am." She picks up one of his pictures and takes a straight blade to it, outlining him carefully before she runs a glue stick over the back and pastes him to the paper in front of her.

"That's so nice of you. That's a beautiful album." I point to the thick book that looks as if it's a giant square and she closes it a moment, proving my theory.

"I picked it up at a specialty shop in Woodley. It's pricey, but I love the iridescent glow."

The album itself is dark purple in hue with a pink and blue patina and it is a real eye-catcher.

"Pretty," I say. "I'm sure his family will love it. I can't imagine what they're going through. Are you doing better?"

"I'll live." She shrugs. "It's weird not having him around, though. I mean, we did practically everything together."

"I bet you were close to Devin then, too. I mean, she was his girlfriend."

She glances to the ceiling. "Yup. She was always there. Popping up when you least expected it. They fought, though."

"They did?" Knew it. My vision is one hundred percent correct. I should probably tell Shep about my sibylline abilities, but then again, he doesn't strike me as open-minded as Opal or Tilly. Not that he's judgmental. It's just that he's a black and white kind of a guy. He was a homicide detective. He's hardwired to look at facts. And face it, my supernatural abilities don't exactly lend themselves to anything factual. It's more or less a hope and a prayer.

She nods. "Oh, they fought all the time. In fact, I just came from the sheriff's department. They wanted to interview me again, and this time I didn't hold back. I told them all about how Devin wanted a baby, and Perry wouldn't give it to her. She said he owed her a kid because she gave him the best part of her life. And that if he didn't do it soon, he would pay for all he had cost her."

I freeze while holding a picture of Shep in my hand. His searing baby blues seem to be looking right at me, and a part of me wonders what it would be like to have babies with someone like him.

A cough sputters from me. "That's, wow, that's terrible. I guess the sheriff's department will be knocking on her door soon enough."

"That's right." Nicki pulls forth a picture from one of Perry's shows. "This is my favorite picture of the two of us."

I squint hard to find her in the picture. "There you are." I point over to her sitting on a stool in the back, seemingly swaying to the music while Perry strums his guitar.

"Nice," I say. "I'm sure he appreciated having you around."

"Are you kidding? I did everything for him. The man couldn't even tie his shoes without me. He needed me." Her chest bucks. "He needed me that night and I was nowhere to be found."

"Hey"—I place my hand on her shoulder—"you were there. You were inside where you belonged. You didn't know he was in any imminent danger. How could you?"

She rolls her eyes. "Well, Devin was present. But to be honest, I didn't see this coming. I thought a breakup was in the works, but a *murder*? You can knock me over with a feather."

She pulls forward another picture and there's a man with prickly facial scruff and I suck in a quick breath.

"Hey, who's that?" I point over at him.

Nicki's expression sours. "Max Edwards. Bleh. He was always hitting on me."

"Funny you should say that, because I saw him hitting on Perry that night, literally and not in that way. They were having a real deal smackdown backstage before Perry went on."

Her face freezes in a somewhat grimace. "I bet they were. It's not the first time Max has come after Perry. Usually I'm front and center for their spats. That's funny." She glances to the ceiling. "I don't remember seeing him there that night. What were they arguing about?"

I shake my head. "I only heard a snippet. The man, *Max*, said something about getting what was his and that Perry had gone too far."

"Yeah, that sounds like the same old song. And ironically, it's a song they were tussling over. Perry's big hit, 'Come Back to Me'? Max says he wrote it."

"Really?" I lean in and take a better look at the guy. "Did he?"

"Who knows? Perry was always going out and getting drunk with his friends. Some of his greatest hits came from those guzzling sessions. I mean, I guess it could've been true. Usually his friends didn't care if they helped him out with a verse or two, but apparently, Max is a struggling artist. He needs every dime. The truth might just lie somewhere in the middle."

"Do you know what this means? If Max was convinced that Perry stole his song, that would give him motive for murder."

"It would?" She glances to some nebulous horizon. "I guess I never thought of it like that. *Huh.* I guess I have something else to tell Detective Grimsley next time we speak."

I nod. "Leave no stone unturned."

A sharp bout of laughter erupts from the next table over, and I look up in time to see two different women seated on Shep's lap, throwing a peace sign to the bevy of phones documenting the shot.

"Hey"—Nicki elbows me in the ribs—"isn't that your man?"

"That would be him."

"It looks as if you have a popular boyfriend, too. But who are we to resist an earthly deity, right?" She cackles, and yet I can't seem to join in on the fun.

Instead, I close up shop and thank her for the chitchat. I head on over to my *man* and pluck him out of the minefield of estrogen and we sail right out the door and back into his truck.

"How'd it go, Sweet Cheeks?" He forces a smile to come and go when he throws out the cheeky moniker.

"Sweet Cheeks?"

"Yeah, our cover was that we were dating, and if we were dating I'd give you a nickname."

"If we were dating and you called me Sweet Cheeks, I'd question your feelings for me, *Honey Bunch*."

He motions for me to speed things up. "Did you glean anything?"

"She gave me more than I asked for. It was like stealing candy from a baby."

I fill him in on what I gleaned about Devin and that baby Perry never gave her. And I fill him in on Max Edwards, too.

"Max Edwards." Shep lifts a finger while staring hard at the woods across the street. "I think I know the guy."

"Great. We'll just track him down and have a little chat with him."

"I'll track him down."

"Not if I do it first."

Shep shoots me a look, and I shoot one right back.

"All right, Bowie. You win." He shakes his head as he fires up his truck. "Why do I get the feeling you always win?"

AN AWFUL CAT-TITUDE

I don't always win. I'm not sure running from my life, *for* my life, qualifies as winning.

But Shep doesn't need to know that.

In fact, Shep doesn't need to know a single thing about me or the booby prizes I've inadvertently won.

14

The next afternoon at the café, I wait until the lunch rush is over before attacking Shep with my shiny new idea.

I traipse on over as a group of soccer moms titters his way as they sip their lattes. Apparently, there is a very real phenomenon that involves Shepherd Wexler's presence and a direct correlation to an increase in female customers. Too bad that increase doesn't pan out to an increase in sales. The numbers are so dismal each night when I count out the drawers, I'm almost afraid to report them to Opal.

"Hey, Shep." I refill his coffee. "Leaded fuel, just the way you like it. How's the book coming?"

Those stone cold blue eyes of his glance my way.

"One chapter done. If I get one more in today, I just might buy myself a pony. What's up, Bowie? I can tell by that look in your eye, you're up to no good."

Surprisingly, I'm not nearly as affronted as I should be.

"You haven't known me long enough to know that look in my eye."

"Trust me," he says, pulling his coffee forward, his gaze never leaving mine. "I've been around you long enough to recognize it."

Tilly pops up. "Shep is basically a human lie detector. He has this strange supernatural ability to read people like nobody's business. Once, I had a teeny tiny secret that was eating me up on the inside, and he called me on it. Of course, after I spoke with him about it, I felt miles better." She sighs dreamily and it begs the question if he had done something else to make her feel miles better, too.

"Nice." Not nice. In addition to hiding my deep, dark secret from Shep—two of them to be exact—it seems I'll have to put on an Oscar winning performance as if to prove I don't have any supernatural skeletons to hide. "I was just going to say that my internet search on Max Edwards didn't yield anything. I thought maybe you could don your detective hat to see if you can find him—and, I promise to stay in the background like you did at the library. Only I don't foresee me being mobbed by hormone-hungry women."

Shep closes his laptop. "I don't need to don my detective hat. I remembered last night where I've seen him before. He's been to a few of my local signings, and he just so happened to be at Maple Grove Community College as a student when I spoke to the creative writing class last week."

"Oh! Great. Let's get back there and talk to him."

"No can do. It's finals week. The semester just wrapped up."

Tilly grunts, "The guy probably has a day job."

Shep nods. "More like evenings. He's a waiter at the Blue Vase in Maple Grove."

"*Ooh.*" Tilly's shoulders dance with glee. "That's a ritzy place. So when are we going?"

"*We?*" I look up at her.

"That's right." Her hot pink lips expand with a glint of mischief. "Men who dine at the Blue Vase obviously have money, and if I'm going to beat Jessie over the head with the mantra *it's just as easy to marry a rich man as it is a broke joke*, then I need to lead by example." She plucks her phone from her purse. "I'll call and see if Max is on the schedule tonight."

"No, don't do that," Shep says just as she zips off.

I shrug over at him. "I haven't been here that long, but I do know you can't stop Tilly once she sets her mind to something."

He gives a sly wink. "You have that in common."

"Hey? You really do know me."

Opal pauses our way, clad in a black leather jacket. Her matching skirt drops off just below the knee, and she's wearing black tights with a herringbone pattern. But it's that furry treasure in her arms that has my full attention. King sits against her chest and looks perfectly content to be burrowing into her leather jacket.

"Opal, you look fabulous," I say. "But it's nearing triple digits out there. Aren't you piping hot?"

Her crimson lips pinch tight. "That's precisely why I don't plan on leaving the manor. The air conditioning is divine. Speaking of which, I just saw the electricity bill. I move we have Stitch Witchery every night of the week."

"That bad, huh?" I wince.

"Worse." She pokes me on the arm with her well-manicured fingernail. "We need more ideas, and fast. I've only got so much comfort to spare."

"Okay," I say. "I'll put on my thinking cap and come up with something great that will put us both in the green, I promise."

Tilly bops over once again. "Guess who's going to dinner tonight at the Blue Vase?"

Opal groans, "I'd love to, dear, but Bowie just pointed out it's Hades out there, and if I begin to glisten, I'll never get this skirt off." She gives a wave with King's paw before heading to the next table.

"Tonight?" I say to Shep as if looking for approval, but I think we both know it was more of a command.

He takes a full breath. "It sounds as if I get to have a little fun with two women tonight at the very same time," he says it with a bona fide frown and I can't help but laugh.

"Oh, come on, Shep," I tease. "I can tell by that look in your eye you've had a little fun with two women before at the very same time. Trust me, I've been around long enough to know this." I give a sly wink of my own as I hand his own words right back to him.

Now to get ready for a ritzy night out.

Max Edwards owes me answers, and I know just the little black dress in my gently used closet that might pull every last confession out of him.

To be honest, when Tilly said the Blue Vase was ritzy, I automatically assumed it was ritzy by Starry Falls' standards, something elegant and classy that required you to take your ball cap off before dinner. But what I wasn't expecting was to feel as if I had just been transported straight to the Upper East Side of Manhattan.

"Wow," I muse as I take in the venue.

The floors are stained a woodsy shade of ebony and the tables gleam of Carrara marble. Moody romantic music seeps from the speakers as elegantly dressed couples take to the dance floor. Every person here is dressed to the nines, men in suits and women in cocktail dresses. And the scent of a perfectly grilled steak is the piece de résistance.

Tilly bumps her arm to mine. "I know, right? It's like prom for adults, only it goes on every single night."

Shep steps in front of me with those intense eyes of his needling into mine.

"You look amazing, Bowie."

Tilly scoffs. "So you've mentioned a time or ten. What about me?"

"You too," he says, not taking his gaze from mine. The irony with Shep's compliments is that he only seems to be getting that much more annoyed each time he gives them to me.

A waitress comes by and seats us near the window. It's a nice, intimate, round table set for three with a votive candle in the middle, and if Tilly weren't here, I think my hormones and my heart would have wanted to believe this was every bit a romantic date with Shep. For that reason alone, I'm a bit relieved Tilly is here. The last thing I need is to get romantically involved with anyone on my way to the Great White North. Not that Shep has any track record of holding down a relationship.

Nora comes to mind and quickly dismantles that theory.

The waitress, a tall blonde with eyes the size of silver dollars, can't seem to pick her jaw up off the floor while gawking at the handsome stunner by my side.

"Can I get you anything? Wine? Appetizers? A key to my condo?" She blinks back to life before whipping out a notepad and quickly jotting something down on it. "Here's my number in the event you need it. Use it," she says that last part like a command before taking off.

Tilly smirks. "Well, at least you got that awkward getting-to-know-you phase out of the way. I say she's a home run."

"We're not here to play ball," I snip as I crane my neck into the crowd. "Oh, look!" A spear of excitement rockets through me. "There he is." I nod behind Shep, and both Tilly and he turn in that direction.

Max Edwards looks dapper in a tuxedo and a white folded hand towel draped over his right arm as he serves dinner to a table not too far away.

"We need to get his attention," I whisper.

Tilly checks her phone. "And I'm going to run out of time if I don't get the attention of one of these sharp-dressed men." She cranes her neck. "It looks as if they're all congregating at the bar. I'll see you kids later."

"Wait," I say, grabbing her by the fingertips before she can get away. "What about dinner?"

"Give me whatever you're having." She wrinkles her nose. "Lobster would be nice." She takes off, and soon the waitress is back and Shep and I put in our orders, surf and turf specials all around.

Shep leans in and that thick, spiced cologne of his ensconces me once again. I confess, there is something about this man's cologne that intoxicates me to unsafe levels. Okay, fine. Everything about this man has the capability to intoxicate me regardless of time or place. It's a wonder that hormonal hive of waitresses that keeps buzzing around our table hasn't sunk a sack over his head and taken him hostage.

"Bowie," he whispers my name low and heated and my insides implode with heat. "He's spotted me. He's on his way over."

My lips part, and before I can say anything, Max Edwards himself is darkening our table. His tan glows against his dress shirt and his hair is neatly slicked back.

"S.J. Wexler." He breaks out into a giant grin. "Hope you don't mind me interrupting your romantic evening to say hello."

"Not at all." Shep smiles back and it looks shockingly genuine. Could I be witness to that single nice bone in his body? "Call me Shep. How's the writing going?"

"Geez." Max inches back. "I can't believe you remember me. This is incredible. It's going great, thanks for asking. I'm still at the outlining phase of my novel, but I'm getting close to hitting the keyboard."

"Remember what I said, the first page is the toughest. Don't be intimidated by a blank page because you will undoubtedly rewrite it many, many times in the process."

Max ticks his head to the side. "I know how that goes."

"Oh?" I lean in. "So you're familiar with the editing process. Do you write anything other than novels?" I press my hand to my chest. "I'm Bowie Binx."

"Bowie Binx." He gives a slight bow. "A beautiful name for a beautiful girl. And, in fact, I do write other things. I'm a songwriter as well."

"Songs?" It comes out with a touch too much enthusiasm. "As in rock music?"

He squints to the ceiling. "More like country or folk."

"Hey"—I lift a finger his way—"I work down at the Mortimer Manor and we just had a folk singer come by. He died that same night, too." I shudder at the thought. "Maybe you've heard of him? Perry Flint?"

Max begins to cough and sputter. "Yes, oh yes. I knew Perry." His cheeks burn bright. "We may not have always seen eye to eye, but he was a good musician. I'm a musician myself. Small-time. No contracts, no bells and whistles like Perry." His jaw stiffens at the thought of Perry's ride on easy street with all of those bells and whistles.

"Well, I'm sure you're great," I say. "His song 'Come Back to Me' was my all-time favorite. Have you heard it?"

Max hardens his eyes over mine. If looks could kill, I'd be dead twice over.

Shep clears his throat. "Max, have you sold any of your songs?"

"No." He lets out an exasperated sigh. He's gone from a crazed angry lunatic to a dejected dreamer in just one breath.

"Please, take a quick seat." Shep points to Tilly's chair, and Max reluctantly fills it. "Did something happen?"

Max gives a quick glance around before leaning in. "It did. I wrote a song and a big-time musician ripped it off. And when I asked for the credit that was due to me, he said he didn't have to give it because the lyrics were merely something we were discussing, nothing more than a verbal exchange."

"Is that true?" I ask.

Max glowers past me a moment. "It's true. But the guy used every word I fed him verbatim."

Shep taps his fingers over the table. "Did you try discussing this with him? Maybe bring up a lawsuit?"

"I did, on multiple occasions—but look, this guy had money. I'm just a struggling musician. I'm not going to lie. It hurt like heck knowing he wasn't going to cut me into something that was mine to begin with."

"Max"—I scoot my seat in a notch—"that singer was Perry Flint, wasn't it? I saw your expression change at the mention of him and you didn't exactly look mournful."

Shep's eyes round out in horror as he looks my way.

Okay, so maybe I could have left off the commentary, but I'm sure Max will appreciate my honesty. Or not.

"You got me there." Max belts out a short-lived laugh. "It was Perry. The guy was borrowing lyrics from friends for years. I guess he never had anyone ask to have the proper credit given to them. I could understand if it was just one line or two, but the guy ripped off my entire song. The worst part was I had no way to prove it. I was trusting that he was an upright kind of a guy, and it turned out he wasn't. He even won a Folkey award for my song. The world would never believe it was mine now." He gives a wistful shake of the head. "So much for that."

Shep takes a breath. "I guess chalk it up to a lesson learned. If it makes you feel better, I've had people rip off entire plotlines of mine and there wasn't a thing I could do about it. I can tell you right now, I know how frustrating it can be. Onward and forward, right?"

"I guess." Max does his best to shrug it off.

I tilt my head his way. "Max, when was the last time you spoke to him about it?"

"Not long ago." He glances to the table with a somber look as if reliving a bad memory. "But I knew it'd be one of the last times I could talk to him about it."

"Why's that?" My heart pounds as if we were about to hear a confession.

"I ran into Devin a few weeks back. Apparently, Perry had some crazed fan that was sending threatening messages about a year back. It was still creeping him out, so he was looking to hire private security."

Shep and I exchange a glance. It's the first time I'm hearing about a crazed fan, and my guess is it's his first time, too.

Max blows out a breath. "Perry is dead now. I guess I will have to move on and let go of the piece of me I ripped out to produce that song. But it won't change the fact each time I hear 'Come Back to Me' I shed a little tear for what could have been."

"Oh my goodness, Max"—I press a hand to my chest, feigning surprise—"that was a huge hit! You have some real talent. And I'm sure sooner than later you'll reap the benefit. Hey, you wouldn't have happened to have been at the manor that night Perry gave his final performance, were you?"

Max's eyes flit around the room as if they don't know where to land next.

"No, actually, I wasn't." He rises from his seat. "Dessert is on me tonight. Enjoy your meals."

No sooner does he take off than our food arrives.

I wait until the waitress takes off before I lean toward Shep.

"He lied about not being at the manor the night Perry was killed. Shep, I saw the two of them in a shoving match myself."

He glances over his shoulder briefly. "I believe you."

"I guess Max has a motive. And the fact he's lying sure does make him look guilty."

Shep nods. "And I'm guessing that's exactly why he doesn't want anyone to know he was there. If he did it, he doesn't want to get caught. If he didn't do it, he doesn't want to be pegged as the killer because he realizes he's an easy suspect."

"Do you think Nora knows about him?" My lips twist when I bring up his ex, but at this point, she's a necessary evil.

"I don't know. But I'll compare notes."

A sullen feeling takes over.

Of course, he will. Shep is probably just looking for an excuse to reignite the flame. I don't see why I should mind. The only thing that should be preoccupying my mind is getting Opal rolling in the green so I can peel off a few bills for myself and fix that deathtrap my Uncle Vinnie stuck me with.

Dinner comes and goes without any hope of sparkling conversation. Tilly trots by with a man leading her to the dance floor and pauses at the table.

"Box that platter of deliciousness up to go for me, would you?" Her suitor nudges for her to hurry. "And hit the dance floor at least once tonight." She shakes her head at Shep. "One song won't kill you."

The music drifts to something slow and melodic while Shep tips his chin and examines me from across the table.

"How about it, Bowie?"

"Oh, I don't—um, I can't...I haven't—"

He rises up and lends me his hand. "Enough with the excuses."

I bite down on my lip as he leads us to the nexus of the dance floor and wraps an arm around my waist, pulling me close.

Shepherd Wexler's chest feels rock hard, as in I could easily spend the next few hours washing my clothes over his abs.

His gaze presses into mine as we move in rhythm to the music, and, dare I say, I see the beginnings of a tiny smile budding on his stubborn lips.

Without putting too much thought into it, my head lands over his shoulder and I close my eyes. For a moment, the world around me fades and it's just Shep and me alone in a universe of our making.

The floor beneath me feels as if it's giving way, and I'm overcome with that warm, fuzzy feeling I get whenever a vision begins to brew, and, sure enough, in my mind's eye I'm staring at a computer screen where I see my ex's ugly mug. Johnny's face just so happens to be his avatar on all of his social media sites. And next to his smug mug are the words, *You're not going to get away with this, Stella. Nobody does this to me and splits. I will hunt you down like an animal. You're going to pay for what you've done to me. You haven't seen the last of me yet.*

I blink up at Shep in fright and struggle to pull away.

"Whoa" —Shep pulls me in close once again—"looks like you fell asleep and had a nightmare."

"Yes"—I pant as I try to catch my breath—"something like that."

Shep, Tilly, and I head back to Starry Falls and Shep gives me a polite nod once he walks me to my door. Either he's too stubborn to dole out a kiss or he picked up on the fact I've been in a very big funk ever since I had that bout of insanity while he was holding me in his arms.

As soon as I crawl onto my cute black and white checkered sofa, I pull out my phone and carefully head over to a few of Johnny Rizzo's social media sites. Sure enough, he's done it. Right there, for all to see, is the very threat my sibylline powers afforded me.

If Johnny Rizzo says he's going to hunt me down, I'm as good as found. Johnny was in hiding twenty-four hours before I ever left town, but to him I'm just a possession. In his eyes, I belong to him. And if he wants me by his side, he won't stop until I'm there. I know where Johnny is. It's where he always is when the greedy gravy is about to hit the fan. He's holing up above his uncle's pizza place in Rhode Island.

So I do the only thing I can do. I call the FBI's anonymous tipline and draw them a map of where to find the cunning little rat.

Goodbye, Johnny.

May we never meet again.

But a part of me knows that's just wishful thinking.

15

In an awful irony, I stopped by the local coffee shop before heading to work at the café. And considering the fact the Manor Café boasts of the world's best coffee, with an oversized sign out front, it should be a hint at what needs to change quickly if we plan on keeping the few customers we have.

The manor looms in the distance as I come up on it, and I can't help but smile at the crooked mansion set on a hill with its pointy spires and cathedral windows. It holds a haunted appeal, and yet I'm not terrified at all of the place. Instead, I find it charming, disarming, and downright homey.

Opal's army of kitties, fifty strong if not a hundred, greets me as I make my way up the stone steps. And behind the large gray castle of a building, I can see the falls in the distance as the glowing water rushes down the rocky crags. Green moss and grass cover the hillside and a smattering of yellow flowers is sprinkled about. Spring is in full bloom and the air is warm and holds the scent of citrus and roses.

Starry Falls is like something out of a fairy tale, and simply being in this place makes me feel as if I'm headed for my very own happily ever after. But, soon enough, Johnny and my entire life back in Hastings blink through my mind and take any thoughts of being happy out right along with it.

I pick up a silver cat with a pink nose and drop a kiss on its forehead. There is something so very relaxing about holding a warm, fuzzy, purring creature, and the last thing I want to do is let go.

As soon as I step inside the café, the scent of bacon lights up my senses. There's nothing like the smell of bacon sizzling on the griddle to make you feel good about the day ahead, especially when you know it's going to start off the right way with something delicious in your belly. The cooks in the back have already whipped up enough pancakes to feed a small island nation, as Mud, the handyman, heads my way.

"Opal wanted me to check up on things." He offers a sober nod.

Why do I get the feeling *check up on things* is code for check up on me?

"You're running out of supplies." He looks to me with those bulging eyes of his, and it's a bit off-putting. "Making sure the café is well stocked was Regina's job. Just saying, you're the new Regina, so you'll have to go and pick up some more stuff before you run out of things to serve the customers."

"No food definitely equals no customers. What do I do? Where do I go?"

He squints out the front windows. "Let's see, Regina made a few runs to Basket Mart a few times a week. Start there."

"Basket Mart?" My own eyes nearly fall out of my head. "As in the supermarket down the street?"

Customers stream through the door all at once, and Shep happens to be one of them. He gives a nondescript wave before heading off to his usual seat.

Tilly runs up and snatches a handful of menus as do Thea and Flo, and just like that, the café is bustling.

"Yup, Basket Mart." Mud gives his scraggly blond mane a quick scratch. "Where else would she get the food for this place?" He takes off for the back, and I take off to the floor to find Tilly.

"Hey, Bowie." Tilly gives me a sly wink as she pours Shep a cup of coffee. "The two of you look a touch grumpy today. I'm betting it has to do with a serious lack of sleep. Might I ask what kept the two of you up late on a hot spring night? A little shared aerobic workout, maybe?"

"Not that," I say. "I just spoke to Mud and he said Regina bought the supplies for this place at the grocery store down the street. Is that true?"

A look of confusion crosses her face. "Why wouldn't that be true?"

"Because it's a good way to go bankrupt. I'll need to find a restaurant supply store. Shep, you have your laptop open. Would you mind looking one up for me?"

His expression goes from affable to ornery in a single bound, but I'm not offended. Ornery is his signature look.

"Your wish is my command, Bowie Binx," he says as he clicks out of the document he's working on, and soon the screen is populated with a jumble of pictures from the internet.

A sharp gasp emits from me as I zero in on one picture in particular.

AN AWFUL CAT-TITUDE

Sitting on the screen, on some generic news site, is Johnny's face front and center with the word *captured* printed in red bold letters right above his smug mug.

Shep glances back at me and pauses. "Everything okay?"

My mouth falls open. "Y-yes." I clear my throat. "I mean, you just said my wish was your command. I probably should have asked for something a little bit bigger."

Tilly plucks the pencil from behind her ear and points it my way.

"Like fixing that car you've got sitting on Main Street?" She bumps her hip to mine. "Hate to be the one to break it to you, but I saw a ticket sitting on your windshield."

"Oh no-o-o." I tip my head back in grief at the thought.

"Hey, Shep?" Tilly looks his way. "Does your brother still own that body shop in Scooter Springs? I bet he'll know someone who can fix it." She leans my way with a devious gleam in her eye. "And after the night the two of you just had, I'd say Shep should be negotiating quite the deal." She shrugs. "His brother has done more for me in exchange for a six pack." She takes off, and to my relief Shep's laptop is already pointing the way to six different restaurant supply stores in the area.

"I'll call my brother." He scowls at the screen. "There's a restaurant supply store out in Woodley." His brows narrow a moment, giving him an otherworldly appeal, and I think Thea just dropped a dish because of it. "Nora called this morning. She invited me out that way. It looks as if they're doing their final inspection of Perry's rental home today."

Every last bit of me tingles at the thought. "And you're extending an invite?"

"No," he flatlines. "But if you need a ride to Woodley to pick up a few things for the café"—he close his eyes a moment—"it's on the way."

"Yay!" I give an odd little cheer. "And, Shep, I really appreciate it."

"I know," he says, getting right back to his work.

I fly to the office in the back and quickly hop onto the internet to see the news for myself.

Johnny Rizzo arrested. Moretti crime family crumbles to dust. Black day for the New Jersey Cosa Nostra.

There would have been a time when reading this would have made me sad, made me angry, and sponsored a ridiculous level of vengeance in me. But right about now, I think I'll have a cookie to celebrate. Johnny Rizzo isn't going to hunt me down because I hunted him down first.

Who knows?

Maybe I'll get that fairy-tale ending after all.

Perry Flint lived in Woodley, on a street lined with maple trees. Each house has its own white picket fence and there are kids riding their bikes up and down the street, while mothers stand in groups, gawking at the police cruisers parked in front of a blue house with a couple of dying pots of foliage set out on the porch.

Shep leads me into the house where we find a handful of sheriff's deputies combing through drawers and files with gloves on. We head into the office in the back where Nora looks up from what looks to be a monthly planner in her hands.

"Well, well"—she pulls a tight smile, that bun in her hair looks even tighter—"I didn't know it was date night. Shepherd, this isn't show-and-tell. And I don't have any spare gloves, so I'm afraid she'll have to leave."

Shep digs into his pocket and pulls out a pair of gloves for both himself and me.

"What do you know?" He looks to Nora. "I happen to have a spare."

She takes a moment to glower at me as Shep pulls on his gloves.

"What did you find?" he grunts her way. It's nice to know his grumpy personality isn't exclusively shared with me.

Nora sniffs. "There are some things in the bedroom we're itemizing. Shep, why don't you have a look with me? Ms. Binx, you stay put until further notice. Don't break anything."

I wait until they leave to pull on my gloves and examine the planner she just put down. It's filled to the brim with dates, with the names of venues I'm guessing Perry was set to perform at.

Judging by the loopy, flowery, handwriting, this was written by a female. Probably Nicki—she's the personal assistant, or at least she was.

I put the book down and glance around the dark room. It's lined with bookshelves, mostly filled with folders, each labeled with a different year. Some are marked *tours*, others marked by the month. I spot a thick iridescent spine up above and do a double take. It looks vaguely familiar, and it's not until I pull it out do I realize it's a scrapbooking album—the exact dark purple hue with an iridescent patina that the album Nicki was working on had.

AN AWFUL CAT-TITUDE

I bet she did this one, too. I open it up and blink back a moment at what greets me. It's a note, pieced entirely of different sized letters that were cut and pasted from magazines and newspapers. *I was in the crowd and you pretended not to see me.*

I turn the page and find another and another, all with the same creepy statements.

Remember to look over your shoulder some time. I'll be there.

Love me not?

I don't like to be ignored.

You will know me soon enough.

"*Huh,*" I whisper to myself. I quickly rifle through the rest of it, only to find it brimming with odd statements. It's chilling to the bone.

"Bowie?" Shep calls from behind, and I nearly jump out of my skin. He heads over, a look of concern rife on his face. "What's this?" he asks, carefully taking the album from me as Nora appears glancing over his shoulder.

"How do you like that?" She sneers my way. "You're here five minutes and you stumble upon a gold mine. And to think, Shep, you said she wasn't exactly a horseshoe."

I frown up at him as Nora takes the book.

"Nora"—I step in—"last night, Max mentioned that Perry has someone who was harassing him—that he was about to get private security for himself."

"This is the first I'm hearing of it." Her eyes enlarge as she looks to the book in her hands. "I'll have to ask around again."

"What about the murder weapon?" I pant as my heart begins to race. My window of time in this place is quickly closing, I can feel it.

Nora takes a breath. "Richard Broadman mentioned Perry had a gun on him at all times. But there was no gun found on the body. Instead, we found an empty holster."

I blink over at Shep. "He was murdered with his own gun? If that's true, I doubt whoever did this was planning it—unless the plan was to use his own weapon against him."

Nora gives a bitter laugh. "You're a little miss know-it-all, aren't you? Do everyone a favor and leave the hard questions to me."

We finish up at Perry's place and head off to the restaurant supply store where I use the money Opal gave me to buy enough ingredients to last through next week.

Shep and I drive back to the manor and park behind the kitchen where Mud comes out to help offload the supplies.

Molly, the fuzzy little teddy bear cat, traipses my way and I scoop her up as I stare off in a daze, trying to digest that creepy album I spotted back at Perry's place.

"You're deep in thought." Shep steps in front of me and sets those daring blue eyes over mine.

I let out a breath. "Nora said that no one mentioned Perry could have had a stalker. I wonder why Nicki or Devin didn't bring it up?"

"Bowie." Shep shakes his head as if to stave off what I'm about to say next.

A little laugh trembles through me. "You really do know me."

I'm not done with Nicki or Devin just yet, and there's nothing Shepherd Wexler can do to stop me.

16

Stitch Witchery was had again, and a jolly good time was had by all—because, well, *whiskey*.

As it stands, just about every woman has something that ails them, thus requiring a sufficient amount of comfort to be added to their tea. Not surprisingly, word has gotten out and we've swelled from one table to three. True to her word, Flo made me a pattern that reads *MEOW*, and next to that word is a grandfather clock with a cute little cat that I'm going to make the exact shade as Molly.

Flo provided me with an Aida cloth and let me borrow one of her hoops, a needle, and has generously given me all the thread, *floss* as she calls it, to finish my project. I'll admit, there's something relaxing about making these detailed little X's that will eventually result in a bigger picture. And once Stitch Witchery ended, I took my new project back to my place to work on in my spare time.

The next day at the café, all through breakfast and straight through the lunch rush, I decide to poll our customers and find out what their favorite menu items are so I know what specials to highlight—so we can run specials in general.

While Shep and I were in the restaurant supply store, I purchased a chalkboard and an easel to set out front as a means to show off our dish of the week—one for breakfast, lunch, and dinner. But as it turns out, our customers decided to eschew the edibles on the menu and overwhelmingly agreed they love Opal, her cats, the shape of our ice, and the ambiance of the café—those last two left me a little more than baffled.

"The shape of our ice?" Tilly gives a few rapid blinks and nearly loses a false eyelash in the process.

I nod to the small group before me. Tilly, Mud, Thea, and Flo have all been included in this little impromptu staff meeting at the counter. Opal is off regaling the customers with King, the Bengal cat who is clearly in charge of this kitty circus, and Derby, a long-haired orange tabby.

"Then it's settled." Mud scoffs and tosses his hands. "There's no way we're getting a new ice machine. The public has spoken."

"Mud." I close my eyes a moment too long. "The ice machine was never up for dispute. I'm thinking of upping our java game with new coffee and espresso machines. But we need to have people talking about our food, too. And since nobody in this town seems to actually care for anything we serve, I thought I'd poll all of you instead. What kinds of food would you like to see on the menu?"

Flo grunts, "Food?" Her dark hair sits on top of her head like a bird's nest and it has an odd blue patina to it this morning. "Try world peace and climate control. Table five needs more ice." She takes off, and I look to the others.

Mud shakes his head. "You're just complicating things, Bowie. Regina never cared about the food here and people still walked through that door." He pats me on the shoulder. "We've given them ice the way they want it. Let's not spoil them." He takes off to the back, and I open my mouth to Tilly and Thea, but before I can get a word out, I give up on the endeavor.

Thea licks her lips. "You know, my Grammy makes a great bologna cake." She shrugs as her auburn hair fringes her eyes. "It's frosted with mayo and sprinkled with pimentos. I'm pretty sure she's taking this recipe to the grave, but if you want, I can try to pry it from her cold, shriveled hands."

My lips seal themselves shut as I examine the ingénue before me. "Fight the good fight, Thea."

She gives a knowing nod before heading back out on the floor.

Tilly gives her hair a quick fluff, disrupting the pattern in her chunky highlights.

"How about you, Tilly? What would you like to see on the menu? And what about Jessie? What's she into?"

"Let's see." She chews on the inside of her cheek as she considers this. "Jessie likes bad boys with a side of adult male convicts, and I do believe she gets that hankering from her mama." A husky chuckle bumps from her. "Good luck getting *that* on the menu." She flips a dishrag over her shoulder as she takes off to seat new customers.

Lovely.

I'll just whip up a vat full of convict soup and bring 'em in by the droves. Little do the customers here know they've already got a wanted felon doling out their daily dishes.

That heavy feeling that's been stalking me begins to seep in and I do my best to shrug it off. I refuse to fall into the pit of my own making. Instead, I make my way over to Opal and Shep.

Opal pulls me in by the arm. "Just the girl we were talking about. It turns out, Shep's brother is coming to town in a bit to see about that car of yours." She squints over at me, and that black eye shadow she's prone to using gives her that raccoon effect I'm pretty sure no woman is after—no woman except for Opal, of course. "Promise me you won't gallivant off into the sunset. The manor needs you. I'm making a killing off Stitch Witchery now, and who knows how many more bursts of financial genius you have lurking around in that head of yours?" Her lips twist into a rather cartoonish pout. "I'm afraid you'll have to stay."

My shoulders bounce in lieu of an answer. There's a niggling part of me that insists I make a run for the Canadian border—the part of me that hates the idea of three hots and a government-issued cot—and yet there's a whole other side of me that says *plant your feet in Starry Falls and let the roots run deep.*

Shep catches my eye and nods as if he heard the whole internal debate and was siding with me building a root system. Of course, knowing Shep, he's actually cheering for me to leave, thus, the fact his brother is coming to town.

"Thank you, Shep. I really appreciate that." I bite down on my bottom lip hard as I look to Opal. "You know all that income we're seeing from Stitch Witchery? I think we should reinvest it into the café."

"What? *No*." Her eyes round out in horror. "And ruin the prospect of wrapping myself in the entire Jill Herrera summer line? Please." Her protest ends with a laugh, but judging by the pained look on her face, you'd think I just suggested we chop off the tails of every cat in Vermont.

"Yes," I insist sweetly. "Opal, with great coffee, we could start seeing real green that makes anything we earn from our comfort tea look like spare change you find in a couch cushion."

Shep's brows sharpen. "Do I want to know what comfort tea is?"

I give a frenetic shake of my head in Opal's direction.

Face it, with Shep's background in law enforcement, he's basically a narc.

"Speaking of comfort." I stretch a quick smile across my face. "I'm taking a poll."

"I heard." He pulls his coffee forward and frowns my way. "Funny, I don't remember you polling me when I walked in."

"That's because you grunted at me when I said good morning. In the event you're not aware, that's tantamount to a *do not disturb* sign. Besides, I really do know you by now. There's no sense in trying to start up a conversation until you've been properly caffeinated." I'm about to ask when he thinks his brother might get here, and just like that, a flood of emotions hits me at the thought of leaving this drafty, crooked manor that I've grown to love.

Shep's lips curl as he examines me. "My brother will be here in a few minutes. I've already told him where to find your car, and he said he'd let me know when he arrived."

"Sounds good." I sigh, pushing all thoughts about leaving Starry Falls out of my mind entirely for now. "Shep, I'm thinking about implementing a few changes around here. Are there any specials you'd like to see as far as the menu goes?"

"You have my vote on the new coffee machine." He winces at Opal. "Sorry." He looks back my way. "And I'm easy as far as food goes. I'm curious to see what you'll come up with."

"I'm curious to see what I'll come up with, too." That warm, fuzzy feeling takes over, tunnel vision sets in, and soon I'm treated to a snippet of the future via my mind's eye.

The ballroom in the back of the manor appears, and Max Edwards is crooning away into a microphone while people sway to the music. And just like that, the vision disappears.

"Oh my goodness"—I pant—"I just had a great idea." It's times like these my visions really are a gift. "We can have a memorial concert for Perry Flint right here at the manor. I bet we can get Max Edwards to perform his songs, and I can ask Tilly to help rustle up a few other local bands."

Opal's ruby red lips make a perfect oval.

"Why, look at you go!" She pats me on the hand. "You are a genius, Bowie Binx. We're available this Saturday. I'll charge a cover of twenty dollars a person, and, of course, we'll have a *comfort* station." She gives a sly wink.

"How about a ten dollar cover with some of the proceeds going to help his family cover funeral costs? That way people won't bat a lash at forking it over."

"Good thinking." She holds up a finger. "And portion can mean anything. I'm thinking cents on the dollar."

Shep's phone bleats. "And he's here."

Opal snaps her fingers my way. "Stay in town, missy. I'm depending on you to whip my finances into shape. Remember, fifteen percent of those are yours." She takes off as Shep places his laptop into his briefcase.

"I guess I get to meet another Mr. Wexler." I bounce on the balls of my feet as Shep stands up next to me. "I wonder which one I'll like best?"

He sheds the hint of a smile, and I think I already know.

The spring sunshine warms our backs as Tilly, Shep, his brother, and I stand next to my beat-up Honda, Wanda, near the tail end of Main Street.

"Leslie, I'd like to introduce you to Bowie Binx." Shep's chest widens as he looks my way. He's wearing a suit, which he seems to do when he's about to head over to Woodley to see Nora. I'd like to think it's because he's doing official business, but I'm afraid Nora might be a very real factor in his dress to impress scheme. "Bowie, this is my brother, Leslie."

"Well hello, Leslie." There are some things you don't mean to say out loud but are even more fantastic when you do.

Leslie Wexler is a tall, beefy drink of water, muscles for days bulging out of his tank top, abs that threaten the very existence of anyone in a ten-foot vicinity, and the same lake blue eyes as his brother. And in contrast to his ornery sibling, he wears a delicious smile.

Both Tilly and I sigh in unison.

"Nice"—he sheds a prideful grin—"you can call me Lee." He looks to Shep. "My brother likes to try to embarrass me a little." He gives a wink my way, and I gasp involuntarily. "But I don't mind. Whatever makes him feel like a big man is fine by me."

Shep averts his eyes as if he wasn't having any of it.

"Let's get the show on the road." Shep motions to poor Wanda who looks as if she's never had a bath in her life. She was faded when Uncle Vinnie gave her to me, but after roasting under the Starry Falls' sun, she's just an idea of the color red.

I quickly hand the keys over to Lee and he dives right under the hood before pulling his tow truck alongside her and employing every resuscitative effort in the book.

Shep nods me over to the shade as we head for the awning underneath the ice cream shop.

He looks through the window. "Are you up for it?"

"I am if you're buying."

We head on in while Tilly does her best to assist Shep's brother—or more to the point, she does her best to distract him.

The ice cream shop is light and bright inside. The walls are pink with pastel polka dots sprinkled all around, and perky music streams in from the speakers. The warm scent of waffle cones takes over my senses and I fight the urge to hop behind the counter and attack the stack of freshly made goodness.

I order a double scoop of pistachio and Shep does the same with rocky road before we head out to the bench in front where we watch *The Lee and Tilly Show* unfold.

"So what have you got, Detective Binx?" Shep taps his arm to mine. "Where are you in your investigation?"

"Right now, my tongue is investigating this pistachio ice cream, thus the licking frenzy ensuing."

"Pistachio isn't your run-of-the-mill flavor. Which makes sense. You're not your run-of-the-mill girl."

"Did you just judge me based on the flavor of ice cream I chose to enjoy?"

"No judging. Just pointing out a fact."

"Okay, fine. I'll spill all I know about the investigation, but only because you pitched for frozen dairy." I blink up at the pristine blue sky. "Let's see, we've got Devin O'Malley. The deceased's ex. She's a bit of a character, but who isn't?" That vision that I had of her comes to mind and I get lost in thought. "There's definitely something up with her, but I can't quite pinpoint it." I can pinpoint it, all right. She confessed. Now all I need to do is get to that point in the future. "She mentioned that Richard and Perry had troubles. Something about Perry booking gigs without Richard's knowledge and that Richard was ticked because he wasn't getting his cut." I shake my head. "I don't know. There's just something about her. I can't put my finger on it. Something isn't sitting right. How about you? Any thoughts on Devin?"

Shep tips his head back. "She was jumpy when I questioned her. Nora said the same thing. She's definitely hiding something."

"Knew it." I quickly lap up as much of my cone as I can before it drips all over my fingers. "Then there's Richard Broadman himself, Perry's manager. I'd definitely call him a bad character. He's a big flirt despite the fact he's very married with children. When I confronted him about his beef with Perry, he said the rumors were true. Perry was running around on him and he didn't like it. At least he got an ounce of what his wife will feel when she finds out he's a hound dog. My apologies to hound dogs everywhere. Anyway, he had a solid motive. He wanted his piece of the pie, and Perry wasn't giving it to him."

"Duly noted." Shep tosses those silvery blue peepers my way and his cheek glides up one side. "Next."

"I don't know. There's Nicki Magnolia, but all she seems to do is help. She's the one scrapbooking a memento for the poor guy's family. Did you ever ask her about that stalker scrapbook we found?"

"Nora said she was sending it out for testing first."

"I see. The wheels of justice spin slowly."

Shep lowers his chin and it feels as if he's pressing his weight against me with those eyes.

"They do, Bowie, but the vehicle eventually arrives at its destination."

A chill rides through me despite the heated temperatures at the thought of Shep arriving at his destination—namely me.

"Max Edwards." I clear my throat. "Poor guy. I can't imagine how frustrating it would be to know that someone hijacked your life's work like that."

"I wouldn't call it his life's work, but nonetheless, not a good feeling. I've actually had a writer or two accuse me of stealing their plotlines, and their novels weren't even published. I get it. People get possessive over what they've created. I'm the same way. And I think for that reason alone, Max will come running to perform at the memorial. That was a great idea, Bowie. And I want to thank you for helping Opal at the café, too." His brows bounce. "I've come to regard her as a somewhat eccentric aunt."

"*Eccentric* is a bit too mellow of a word when it comes to describing her. That ex of hers must have really done a number on the poor girl."

"She had it all and she lost it. Her old life disintegrated before her very eyes, and she was forced to start over right here in Starry Falls."

A dull moan comes from me. "Boy, can I ever relate." I finish up my cone before pulling my phone out. "If you'll excuse me, I have a memorial to pull together."

I head off around the corner in hopes to call Devin first. But since I don't have her number, I leave her mine with the bartender at the Tumbleweed Tavern and ask her to call me back when she has a chance.

Next I text Nicki, who thankfully slipped me her card that first night. I send a lengthy message about the gathering for Perry and let her know she's welcome to invite her siblings, friends, and anyone else she can think of.

I don't have Max's number, but I call the Blue Vase and ask for him and, sure enough, he's there. I let him know who I am and what I'm after and he's more than thrilled to accept the booking. He doesn't ask for cash in return. He's just thrilled to sing his own songs for a crowd of people.

My phone pings and I glance to the screen and it's a resounding yes from Nicki. The dancing ellipses ignite again and another message pops up. ***Lol! No siblings, but I can rustle up a few friends to haul along with me. I'll bring some posters from his latest promo package and a couple of his personal belongings that I think his fans might appreciate.***

I text right back and let her know that will be great.

My phone rings in my hand and it's an unknown number.

"Hello?" I glance over and see Shep taking off his suit jacket and rolling up his dress shirt.

If I didn't think this day could get any hotter, boy, was I wrong.

"Hi!" a cheery female voice pipes up from the speaker. "Is this Bowie Binx? This is Devin O'Malley. You called and left a message for me at the Tumbleweed Tavern?"

"Yes! Hi, Devin. I wanted to let you know we're hosting a memorial concert for Perry this Saturday at the manor. We have local musicians already lined up, and Nicki is bringing a few posters and personal effects for the fans to enjoy. We'd love to have you there, and please invite anyone, especially Perry's mom and dad, his siblings. Heck, invite your parents and siblings, too."

"This is so very sweet of you. I'll ask his dad and sister, but I doubt they'll come. They're still lost in grief. He lost his mom years ago. And I don't have any siblings myself, but I'll be there, for sure."

"Great. We'll see you there."

We hang up and I blink down at my phone.

Wait a minute. She does have a sibling. She has Bud. He was with her the night of Perry's death and he was with her at the Tumbleweed where I met up with her.

Another thought hits me.

Hey, didn't Nicki bring up something about a sister, while we were doing that mass picture cut and paste session? In the text she just sent, she mentioned that *she* didn't have any siblings.

Maybe *siblings* was too fancy of a word. Or maybe they're too lost in grief to realize which way is up. Regardless, I'm glad Perry's memorial is fleshing out.

Now to flesh out the killer.

17

Saturday night arrives quick as a lightning bolt.

The manor is elbow to elbow with bodies, all trying to jam their way into the dimly lit ballroom in the back. Meanwhile, King and his kitty cohorts are wisely steering clear of the situation. I saw him lead the charge to the mysterious upper level of this dark and dank haunted house, and I couldn't blame them. In fact, a part of me wanted to join them.

The ballroom is filled to capacity, and I know for a fact Opal charged *fifteen* dollars a person, which is five over what we agreed upon, but I won't complain. After all, I do get a portion of it.

Tilly clip-clops her way over in sky-high heels and a silver sequin dress that might actually be a not-so-long T-shirt of some kind.

"Bowie, Bowie, *Bowie*." Tilly gives my hands a quick squeeze. "This place looks fabulous and so do I." She gives a little spin and the spotlight up above turns her into a human disco ball. "All right, you look hot, too." She gives my little black dress a quick pinch.

"Thanks. It probably once belonged to Regina in another life, but it's mine now. I have the receipt."

She bumps her shoulder to mine before nodding over to Shep.

"That guy once belonged to Regina, too, but take it from me, he has your name on him now." She leans in close to my ear. "You've got the receipt for that, too." She gives a little wink before woo-hooing her way into the crowd, fist pumping while moving her hips to the music.

My eyes stray over to Shep, where the women flock to him freely, touching his clothes as if he were a modern day fertility idol. He glances my way and does a double take, those lids of his dropping down a notch, his lips curling at the tips.

I turn away, trying to play it off as if I were looking for someone else as Opal jogs up. She's donned a black and white striped number that shimmers like water as she moves.

"Bowie Binx!" she blurts my name out in my face as if it were a curse. "I could kiss you on the lips." She grabs ahold of my cheeks and air kisses either side of my face. A much better alternative if you ask me. Especially considering she's wearing blood red lipstick that looks as if it could leave a stain for a decade or two.

"I take it we did pretty well?"

"Are you kidding? We're in the money! We're in the money!" she sings at alarming octaves, and I gently reel her in.

"Considering this is a glorified wake, I'd keep the merrymaking about our profits to a minimum." I lean in. "We'll have tea and cuddle with kittens later. It will be bliss for all involved."

She gives a hard blink. "That does sound like bliss. I think I'll start now." She turns around and heads right out of the room.

I'm about to head toward the stage just as Shepherd Wexler steps in my path. He's donned a dark dress shirt that sets off his eyes, and he looks like the exact mighty fine snack this boy-hungry girl is dying to take a bite out of.

"Bowie." He offers a quick nod.

"Shep." I turn my ear his way.

"You look nice." His eyes remain pinned on mine, and every cell in my body floods with heat.

"Thank you. You don't look so bad yourself." I lean in. "You do realize only you can say *nice* as if it were a four-letter word."

His lips twitch as if they were openly defying him and trying to smile on their own volition.

I shake my head over at him. "Why are you such a tough nut to crack?"

He inches back. "I'm not a tough nut to crack." His brows hike a notch. "Why are *you* such a tough nut to crack?"

A laugh gets caught in my throat. "I guess you got me there."

Shep takes a step in close and a moment pulses by with his eyes locked over mine. My heart drums wildly in my chest and I can't seem to catch my next breath.

In an instant, my body gets that old familiar warm and tingly feeling, and I'm afraid Shepherd Wexler does not sponsor it this time. The room sways in and out of focus and I stumble a moment.

"Bowie?" Shepherd steps in and takes ahold of me by the arm, but it's too late. The tunnel vision has taken over and the noise from the room quickly drowns out as a picture forms in my mind's eye.

A familiar scene begins to appear in what looks to be the café. I'm standing behind the counter just as Shepherd comes up and says something, but I can't quite hear it. Then he sheds a slow spreading smile that I've never seen before.

The room comes crashing back into focus, the horribly loud music accosts my ears, and I take a few quick breaths as if I just jogged to the falls and back.

Shepherd Wexler smiled at me. Or at least he *will*.

I look up at him. Maybe there's hope for us after all?

"Shepherd Pie!" a seemingly inebriated brunette jumps up on his hips and the two of them spin around in a fit of inertia. And just like that, Regina Valentine has whisked him off into the crowd.

"Bowie?" a female voice shouts over the music, and I glance around until I spot Nicki waving at me. Her hair hangs loose around her shoulders. She's got on bright red lipstick and a little black dress that rivals my own. "Sorry I'm late." She cringes while glancing at the box in her arms.. "I wish I could say there was traffic, but the truth is, I got emotional while putting this stuff together."

"I'm sorry." I wince. "Let me help you with that."

"Oh no, it's okay. I ran into Richard in the parking lot and he's right behind me with another box just like this one."

The older gentleman with a shock of white hair comes up behind her and we exchange a cheery greeting.

I have them put the boxes down on a side table I've cordoned off as Nicki and Richard set out the goods. A couple of framed pictures, a stack of his journals, a letterman's jacket, and several awards are among the memorabilia. One of the awards looks like an old-fashioned record player with a large brass horn rising from it, sort of like a Grammy but a little less polished. A few of the triangular awards are made of crystal and catch the light like a prism.

Richard leans our way. "Is that Max Edwards taking the stage?"

I turn to look, and Max enters the limelight with a warm applause from the audience. He's donned a black ten gallon hat and has an acoustic guitar strapped to his chest, looking every bit like the man of the hour.

"That's him," I say as Max begins an old familiar tune, and I recognize it right off the bat as "Come Away with Me".

Nicki swoons to the music. "Wow, he's really knocking this one out of the park." She strides right up to the front of the stage like a woman possessed, and I can't help but give a little laugh.

"He's really that good," I say.

Richard ticks his head to the side. "I guess it would be tacky for me to ask if he needed an agent, but I never said I was above being tacky." He gives a mournful smile.

"Richard, what do you think happened to Perry Flint the night he was killed?" I don't waste any time. I go in full force, no niceties involved.

"I don't know." He shakes his head and gives a mournful smile. "I mean, he had trouble before. He had threats. I guess we didn't take them as seriously as we should have."

"So you know about the stalker?"

Richard looks momentarily surprised. "That I do. Perry had his fair share of crazies. Always coming around, getting too close, sending cryptic messages—the typical stuff a singer of his caliber might see. Surprising, though, to think that one of those nutjobs might have gotten to him in the end."

"Why is that?"

"I'd say it was pretty quiet for the last solid year." He tips his head toward the stage as we watch Max do what it looks as if he were born to do. "Excuse me."

He takes off and I watch the crowd as they hold up their cell phones and illuminate the otherwise darkened room, and it's a magical display—a magical tribute.

I do a quick scan of the room for Shep. I can't help it. I felt something tonight. Something electric, and I wonder if he felt it, too?

If that vision of mine was any indication, something special is about to happen between the two of us. Someway, somehow, Shepherd Wexler is going to give me a genuine smile. And I can't wait to bask in its glory, under its *warmth*.

I spot a blonde ducking into the hall that leads to the backstage area and it looks as if she's being dragged forcefully by someone in front of her. I hike up on my tiptoes and spot the wide frame of a man.

I do another quick scan for Shep but don't see him. And I'm not waiting around to find him either. That woman might be in very real danger.

The last time Perry Flint went down that hallway—he didn't come back.

My feet carry me in that direction before I can process what's happening. The back door is still shut, so I head into the only other room there is, the green room.

I burst in and flick on the lights, only to find a man and a woman jumping apart, both very much surprised, both very much—*related*?

Devin looks right at me, panting, her hair and clothes disheveled, and next to her stands an equally disheveled Bud.

"Devin?" I take a few ambling steps into the room. "Why do I get the feeling this isn't your brother?"

The blonde pants hard, and for a solid second, I'm convinced she's about to pass out.

That phone call we shared earlier in the week comes back to me. Devin knew exactly what she was saying. She doesn't have any siblings—certainly not a brother.

"Oh my God," the words fumble from me. "You're not related at all! You were cheating on Perry with this man, weren't you? In fact, you were doing it right in front of his face. That's so vile I can't even wrap my head around it. How do you sleep at night?" A dull laugh scoffs from me. "Don't answer that. I'm guessing he keeps you up."

Bud groans, "Come on, Devin. We don't need to listen to this. Who does this chick think she is, anyway?"

"I'm your worst nightmare." My mother was right. You can take the girl out of Jersey, but you can't take the Jersey out of the girl.

"Okay, fine," she shouts my way. "You caught me. I'm guilty. Are you happy? Perry left me no choice. I had to do it. He forced my hand. And you're not going to tell anyone, you hear me?" She pauses long enough for me to realize my vision just came to fruition. "Bud, would you give us a minute?"

He shoots me a disparaging look before storming out the door. "Be out in five, Devin, or I'm coming back in. I knew we shouldn't have come back to this place." His voice fades as he drifts down the hall.

"Did you do it?" My heart wallops in my chest. "Did you kill Perry Flint?"

"What?" She inches back as if I struck her. "No! Why would I kill Perry? He was my meal ticket, not to mention the open bar policy his name granted me, and free access to the greatest shows on the planet. Plus, I got to bring my boyfriend along for the ride."

I give a few quick blinks as I try to piece together the information Nicki gave me.

"You wanted a baby and Perry wouldn't give it to you. That's why you went out and found Bud, isn't it?"

She grimaces as if the thought repulsed her.

"Okay, first of all—" Her hand cuts the air, and suddenly it really does feel as if I'm back in Jersey. There's not nearly enough hand gesticulating going on in other states per capita as there is in Jersey. "I'm not a fan of those pint-sized creatures. Heck, I wasn't a fan of them while I was one. And second of all, I didn't pick up Bud after I dated Perry. I came into the picture with him. And before you go and get all high and mighty with me, I don't come from much, so the life Perry was able to afford me was a jewel in the desert of my life. I enjoyed my time with Perry." Tears swell in her eyes. "He was special to me. I don't care what you think of me. I loved him in my own way."

"Yeah"—I scoff—"for what he could give you."

Her jaw stiffens as she barrels past me and I follow her back out into the ballroom where people are still swaying to the rhythm of Max and his acoustic guitar.

Devin heads to the table with Perry's things laid out and her chest bucks with emotion as she looks at them.

I stride up beside her. "You didn't love Perry. You were two-timing him right to his face," I say just loud enough for her to hear. "I'm surprised you were able to keep your story straight."

She clucks her tongue. "What is that supposed to mean? I had two boyfriends, and believe me when I say, I knew which one was which. The math wasn't all that hard." Something on the table catches her eye, and she takes in a never-ending breath. "Oh my goodness, would you look at this?" She picks up the brass knockoff of a Grammy. "It's Perry's old coveted Folkey award. Where did you get this?" The look of surprise on her face dissolves from delight to horror. "Oh my God, they're here."

"Who's here?"

"Whoever swiped this from him a few years back." She shakes her head. "I need to find Bud. I don't feel safe." She takes off and I pick up the Folkey award and run my finger over the large brass instrument welded to the base.

Someone was stalking Perry Flint.

According to Richard, they stopped about a year ago.

Devin mentioned this was Perry's coveted award. Does she really believe Perry's old stalker showed up tonight?

I glance across the room as I feel the heft of the award in my hand and my eyes grow wide. There's a certain someone who just might have the answer.

And maybe, just maybe, they might be the killer.

18

The music grows louder and the noise from the crowd only seems to rival anything that's coming from that stage. The dim lights give the room a smoky appeal, and there are far too many bodies compressed in the ballroom for me to make out anyone's face, let alone find Shep.

But I do see someone I'm interested in speaking with.

I thread my way through the tangle of limbs until I come upon a svelte brunette, her eyes misty with tears as she listens to Max finish up Perry Flint's runaway hit, "Come Back to Me".

"You wish he could come back to you, don't you?" I say it just loud enough for her to hear, and her eyes cut to mine.

Her lips quiver as she gives a hearty nod.

"Yes, I do."

Nicki Magnolia looks lovesick in the very worst way. And I'm betting she is.

"Nicki, what do you know about Perry Flint's stalker?"

"What?" she hisses as she takes a quick look around. "I don't know what you're talking about."

"Did Perry have a fan who was sending him threatening messages?"

Her mouth falls open as she examines me as if seeing me for the very first time.

"I don't think I know about that."

Max starts in on another song, and Nicki does her best to sway to the music.

"Yes, you do know," I say, stepping in front of her in an effort to block her view. "That scrapbooking album you were making for Perry's mother? It was the same kind of album that was found in his office. It had all of these crazy letters, cut and pasted from newspapers and magazines, that somebody pieced together. Each one was a threat issued to Perry. It was put together in the same way you put your scrapbook together. Somebody put those letters in there." A thought comes to me. Nicki said she was making that scrapbook for his mother—but...

Her gaze quickly ping-pongs around the room.

"I have to get some air." She bolts through the crowd and down the hall until she's out the back door and I'm right there with her.

"Nicki, wait," I call out as I step into the chilled night air. "Nicki, you said you were making that scrapbook for his mother."

"And?" Her voice hikes an octave. "So what? I was doing something nice for the poor woman."

"When I spoke with Devin and asked her to invite Perry's parents to tonight's event, she said—she said his mother died years ago."

She takes in a quick breath. "Are you trying to pin something on me?"

"Come to think of it, when I called you the other day, I asked you to invite your siblings and friends, but you said you didn't have any siblings."

"And I don't."

"Then why did you tell me at the library that day you had a sister?"

"I never said that." Her eyes grow wild as she turns to bolt and I snatch her by the wrist and yank her back.

"Yes, you did. You mentioned that your sister was the big scrapbooker in the family and she told you about the event at the library. But that's not true. Nicki, you've been working for Perry for the last solid year, haven't you?"

She pulls her hand free. "What in the world does that have to do with anything?"

"Everything," I say as I pull forward that heavy brass award of Perry's in my hand. "Richard said that Perry had a crazed fan that was sending threatening notes, but that it all stopped about a year ago. Right when you came onto the scene. I bet you were thrilled the day Perry pulled you into his inner circle."

"So what?" Her chest heaves violently. "You can't prove anything."

"This award in my hand might." I hold it up for her to see and she closes her eyes with the sheer look of regret on her face. "You stole it. It had disappeared a long time ago, and yet you magically had it among his mementos tonight. Perry is dead. And my guess is you killed him. Why did you do it?"

"It was Devin, I told you." Her voice hikes up a notch and sends something fluttering out of the evergreens behind us.

I take in a sharp breath. "Yes, you did. You said Devin wanted kids. And they fought because Perry wouldn't give them to her." I shake my head. "But Devin told me, point-blank, she doesn't ever want children—that she's not a fan of those pint-sized creatures. Nicki, you lied."

She starts to take off, and I snatch her by the back of her dress. Nicki trips and stumbles to the ground, taking me right along with her.

"Get off of me!" she riots as she struggles to rise, but I manage to pin her down with my elbow. "So what if I lied about Devin? Who cares about that ridiculous girl?"

"You did lie about Devin," I pant as I search the ground as if looking for clues. "Oh my God, it was you who wanted children! You wanted to have Perry's kids, and he wouldn't give them to you. You were obsessed with him, and it wasn't enough that you got to work alongside him. You wanted him as your own in every way."

"I did." She closes her eyes and winces as if the truth hurt to verbalize. "I loved him. And I knew that he would love me. He said he tried, but that I wasn't the one for him. I gave him everything. But he wanted *Devin*. She's just using him. He came out for fresh air that night of his show, and I followed him. We had an argument. I tried to tell him that Bud is Devin's boyfriend, not her brother, and he *laughed* at me. He said I was a nutcase. He said I couldn't have him. He said I could never have him. I tried to hold him and he pushed me away. I went for him a second time and my hand hooked onto his gun. I was out of my mind with grief. If I couldn't have him, nobody could. So I killed him."

A breath expels from me.

A confession. I'm not sure why, but it's more than I was expecting tonight.

"You're going to tell the detective exactly what you told me."

"I'm not speaking." She gives a little laugh. "And unfortunately, you'll be unable to say a single word—ever again." She snatches the lumbering award from my hand and bashes me over the head with it before I can process what's happening.

A horrid groan comes from me as the pain ricochets long after she stops.

I try to reach for the brass statue just as she's about to crash it down over me once again, but I catch her wrist instead and we struggle for it.

"You don't knock me over the head and get away with it," I grit the words through my teeth as we wrestle it out. Nicki turns me over and pins me to the ground. And just as she's about to deliver another blow with that brass bruiser, I buck her off and the statue goes flying.

I pop to my feet and land my foot over her back just as a small crowd thunders in this direction.

"Bowie!" Shep roars as he reaches for his gun, and Opal, Tilly, and Richard Broadman come running out after him.

"She confessed." I take a stumbling step back as Nicki starts to crawl away on her hands and knees. But Shep has her in his arms and handcuffed before I can catch my next breath.

"She killed Perry Flint," I say as she turns my way, tears streaming down her face. "She was the stalker. She admitted everything. She used Perry's gun to kill him."

Nora Grimsley appears with her weapon drawn, and in just a few minutes, the place is crawling with sheriff's deputies.

Opal shuffles over and lifts my chin with her finger. "You're a keeper, kid. Don't expect a raise." She gives a little wink before heading back inside.

Tilly hops over. "Don't worry, Bowie. I know where she keeps the good stuff. You want me to pour you a stiff one?"

I shake my head. "But thanks for the offer."

She pulls me in for a quick embrace. "You're a tough cookie, Bowie Binx. I'm glad you're one of the good guys." She takes off, and I think about her words.

I'm not one of the good guys.

I'm one of the bad guys on the run.

Nora takes off with Nicki, and I spot Richard talking to one of the sheriff's deputies.

Shep steps up with his hands in his pockets, and those eerie glowing eyes of his are pinned on mine.

"You okay?"

"I'm great." It comes out without the proper enthusiasm. "I suppose you want me to apologize for interfering in your case."

He shakes his head. "No apology necessary. It's over. I'm a big believer in forgetting the past and moving on."

I close my eyes a moment.

My God, how I wish the whole world felt that way. But would I really want to go back to Hastings?

When I arrived in Starry Falls, I thought *this* was the backward upside-down world. And now that I've spent a little time here, soaked in the freedom and the beauty of this place, I'm starting to believe it was the other way around.

A hand warms my arm, and I open my eyes to find Shep's lips curled as he nods my way.

"Let me take you home."

Shep drives me back to the cabin and walks me to the door.

"Bowie?" I look back before heading inside. "If you need anything, anything at all, I'm right next door. Come by anytime. Any hour." He nods as if beckoning me to do so.

"Thank you," I whisper. "Goodnight, Shep."

I head inside, but I don't go to bed. I can't sleep, so I work all hours into the night on that little gift I'm making for my Uncle Vinnie and I finish the very last stitch just as dawn breaks.

I'm safe.

Meow.

19

I did it.

Less than a day after Nicki Magnolia's arrest, I came up with an idea that landed both Opal and me swimming in a sea of green.

I was in the library, holding Molly and petting King, with an entire swarm of attention-hungry kitties corralled around me, when a lightning bolt struck.

Cats in the library.

What on earth could possibly be more inventive than that?

I would have paid money to spend time cuddling up with a furry friend. Curling up with a good book would simply be a bonus. And speaking of bonuses, instead of demanding a cover charge for our new event, the way Opal insisted, I suggested a donation jar to help care for the cats. And judging by the way it's been filling up and overflowing, the cats, Opal, and I will all be taken care of nicely. The cats won't mind sharing. It's only fair Opal and I get our cut.

So today, Opal has opened the doors to the manor library for its very first reading with cats program. For three hours every day, people of all ages are invited to sit and lounge in the manor library and chase down all the cute kitties while reading some good books.

We even went a step further and got the local library to bring out a couple of rolling carts of an assortment of books. The cozy mysteries seem to be a favorite among the Stitch Witchery crowd, and there are enough thrillers, young adult, and chapter books to appease just about everyone. But the real stars of the show are the furry creatures filling every nook and cranny of this place. Tails are whipping around with glee, while the sound of purring amplifies throughout the room.

Flo and Mud are manning the literary fort, so I head back to the café where I spot Tilly talking to Lee.

"Bowie Binx." Lee grins, and ironically it's the only time he actually doesn't resemble his brother. Other than the sexy grin, they're just about interchangeable.

He pulls a set of keys out of his pocket and dangles them before me.

"Your chariot awaits. I took her for a spin, and even topped the tank off for you." He lands the keys in the palm of my hand, hot as flames.

"Oh my goodness," I say as I close my hand around them. "Thank you. How much do I owe you?"

His shoulders jerk. "Seeing that my brother considers you a friend, I'll let it slide this time. But be good to Wanda." He gives a little wink. "And she just might be good to you."

"Thank you." I blow out a breath as I look at the keys in my hand. Right now, they're a portal to another universe entirely, and yet not a single part of me wants to go. I packaged up that pillow I made for my Uncle Vinnie and addressed it to the pizza shop he owns. I could drive to Woodley and mail it before heading up north and getting lost in Canadian mountains, thick with pines.

Tilly snaps her fingers in front of my face.

"Earth to Bowie?" she hums. "I said we're bugging out. Lee's taking me to Granby for dinner. Jessie is with her dad, and I am free for the entire weekend." She takes up his hand

and swings it. "We're ducking out of the country for a little not-so-friendly getaway. Cover my shift, would you?"

"Granby, Canada?"

"Yeah, Quebec." She frowns slightly. "Are you okay?"

"Oh yes. A thought just came to me." I nod her to the side. "Would you mind if I gave you something to drop in the mail for me once you got there? I'm sending an old friend a little something. And you know what? I bet they would be thrilled if it came all the way from Canada." I pull a few too many bills out of my pocket. "Keep the change."

"You better believe I will." She snatches it from me with glee as I quickly retrieve the package for her.

They take off, and I breathe a sigh of relief.

It's happening.

I've made my decision, and I'm not running off to Canada anytime soon. I don't see the harm in staying in Starry Falls for a little while longer—maybe even forever.

I head behind the counter, taking a few orders, and as soon as I finish up with the customers, Shep strides in, looking sharp in a dark blazer and a tie that matches his pale eyes.

He's heart-stopping in just about every capacity, and how I hate that my heart demands to stop in homage of his good looks.

But it's more than that. I like Shep as a person. And if I'm really honest with myself, I'm falling for him—*hard*.

"Well, well, if it isn't Shepherd Wexler," I tease.

"Well, well"—a slow spreading smile takes over his face just the way it did in my vision the other night—"if it isn't Stella Santini."

The smile drops from both his face and mine.

And just like that, I may never have anything to smile about again.

A Note from the Author

Thank you for reading **An Awful Cat-titude (Meow for Murder 1).**

Look for **A Dreadful Meow-ment (Meow for Murder 2) coming up next!**

If you enjoyed this book, please consider leaving a review at your point of purchase. Even a sentence or two makes a difference to an author. Thank you so very much in advance! Your effort is very much appreciated.

Acknowledgements

Hello friend! Thank you so much for coming along to Starry Falls. We hope you enjoyed Bowie's adventure as much as we did. Don't miss book two, MEOW FOR MURDER, **A Dreadful Meow-ment** coming up next. Shep and Bowie certainly have a lot to talk about.

Thank you so much from the bottom of our hearts for taking this roller coaster ride with us. We cannot wait to take you back to Starry Falls!

Special thank you to the following people for taking care of this book—Kaila Eileen Turingan-Ramos, Kathryn Jacoby, Jodie Tarleton, Margaret Lapointe, Ashley Daniels and Lisa Markson.

A heartfelt thank you to Paige Maroney Smith for being so amazing in every single way.

And last, but never least, thank you to Him who sits on the throne. Worthy is the Lamb! Glory and honor and power are yours. We owe you everything.

About the Author

Bellamy Bloom

Bellamy Bloom is a **USA TODAY** bestselling author who writes cozy mysteries filled with humor, intrigue and a touch of the supernatural. When she's not writing up a murderous storm she's snuggled by the fire with her two precious pooches, chewing down her to-be-read pile and drinking copious amounts of coffee.

Visit her at:

www.authorbellamybloom.com

Addison Moore

Addison Moore is a **New York Times**, **USA Today**, and **Wall Street Journal** bestselling author who writes mystery, psychological thrillers and romance. Her work has been featured in **Cosmopolitan** Magazine.

Previously she worked as a therapist on a locked psychiatric unit for nearly a decade. She resides on the West Coast with her husband, four wonderful children, and two dogs where eats too much chocolate and stays up way too late. When she's not writing, she's reading. Addison's Celestra Series has been optioned for film by **20th Century Fox.**

Feel free to visit her at:

www.addisonmoore.com